The "Code of the Blue" is to what the police officers go by. It not only involves protecting and to serve the public but to protect and serve their own in blue. This code is taken seriously and in some cases used against the law itself.

There are 99.99% good police officers in the country, the .01 % are the ones we see on TV beating blacks. It seems that white police officers are always beating blacks. Black police officers know that if it were the other way around they would be the ones prosecuted and convicted of their acts.

Just because men put on the blue uniform doesn't mean

They are exempt from the law but must serve the law.

What happens when the police officers form a society to rid their own department from an unwanted group within the department?

Lieutenant Jonathan Wolfgang Wilhelm has the task of finding the vigilante group known as the "Blue Society," that is ridding their own department and possibly other departments as well of this unwanted group.

Lieutenant Wilhelm or "Wolf" as he has become known with in the force must find and bring to justice the Society that runs deep within the department in Chicago.

The Blue Society

A.W. Hopkins

iUniverse, Inc.
Bloomington

The Blue Society

iUniverse books may be ordered through booksellers or by contacting:

iUniverse
1663 Liberty Drive
Bloomington, IN 47403
www.iuniverse.com
1-800-Authors (1-800-288-4677)

ISBN: 978-1-4401-3896-6 (sc)
ISBN: 978-1-4401-3897-3 (dj)
ISBN: 978-1-4401-3895-9 (ebk)

Printed in the United States of America

iUniverse rev. date: 07/12/2011

Prologue

As Linda was growing up she realized that there was some thing different about her. She was always wanting to play house but never having a daddy figure. There were always just girls and playing with her dolls. Having a collection of Barbie dolls and never had wanted a Ken doll.

As she got older not wanting to be around boys or dating them just to go out and have fun but nothing serious. The boys would always say she was different and call her names when she would only let them kiss her on the cheek after a date.

After graduating from high school Linda and some of her friends decided to apply for law enforcement jobs that were open to the public.

A. W. Hopkins

After her and three others of her friends were accepted they were off to the Law Enforcement Academy and training to be in the police department of Chicago.

No one would know their little secret . . . until.

Part 1

This book is dedicated to my mother. I know she would be proud of my accomplishment.

One

Linda graduated in the upper 10 percent of her class and wanted to go to the police academy.

She had always wanted to be in law enforcement and hoped she could talk to her friends about it.

That night the four of them met and discussed various topics including law enforcement.

One of them said. "I never thought much about it."

Linda said. "They make pretty good money and you don't have to worry about getting laid off."

Another one spoke up and said. "What does it take to get into the academy anyway?"

Linda replied. "There are tests to take and you have to fill out an application."

"Do you think we could all get into the police academy and be accepted Linda?" one of them asked.

"Let's check online first, that way we won't have to go down town."

They went over to the computer and booted it up and logged on.

Linda found the web site she was looking for and the rest of the group looked over her shoulder as the web site popped up. There was an address for online applications to be sent out.

Linda typed in the four addresses for their applications.

A couple of days later they all met again and had their applications with them. They carefully filled out them and then compared them to each others.

The week went by slowly and Linda happened to check her mail this time instead of her mom. There was a brown envelope with her name on it from the city of Chicago. Linda opened it and was surprised that her application had been accepted.

She ran into the house full of excitement. Her mom was standing in the kitchen and Linda ran over and showed her mom the letter.

"I'm so proud of you." Linda's mom said and gave her a big hug. "Wait until your father hears about this."

Linda ran to the phone and called her friend.

"Did you check your mail yet?" she asked her.

"No the mail hasn't come yet. Why?"

"I received my application back and it has been accepted. I'll call you back later."

Later all of the other friends had received their applications back and were informed when the tests would be given.

That night when they met they jumped and carried on. They now had to pass the tests that were going to be given in two days.

They all gave each other a hug.

Two

The tests were going to be given at the local university at two pm.

Linda and her friends had a good idea what some of the questions consisted of from a friend of hers.

That day there were about sixty people taking the tests.

They all looked around and Linda said. "I never dreamed they're would be this many taking the test. I wonder how high a score it will take to pass?"

The tests were passed out and a time limit was set for each one.

They left after completing the tests with a good feeling about the tests. They were told that forty positions were open for this session in the Police Academy.

They got word back that they were all accepted and to report to city hall to fill out the necessary paperwork before going to the academy.

There was one man there watching as they processed their paperwork. He gave Linda a weird feeling.

When they arrived at the academy it there was a lot of yelling from the instructors to fall into line. One of her male friends was slow getting off the bus and an instructor came over and got in his face. He started yelling, and spit was coming out of his mouth and landing on him.

The days went by and the group stuck together. They realized there was another one like them so they asked him to join their group.

For some reason it seemed like one of the five was always being picked on. It was more often than any of the others.

One night they all got together and went over some of the things they observed.

"Why is it we're being singled out more than others do you suppose?"

"You don't suppose they know about our group do you?"

"I don't see how they could." Linda said.

"Have any of you noticed a man coming around and watching everybody?"

Someone said he's with the police department and wants to watch the recruits."

"Every time I see him he gives me the creeps." Linda said.

Graduation day they all were in their police uniforms and looking at each other and making comments on how nice each other looked.

They received their diplomas and were given their assigned precincts to report to.

The man was present at graduation and watched them all receive the diplomas.

Linda was assigned to the One O Five precinct in the Cicero district. The others were assigned elsewhere within Chicago.

Right now all they wanted to do was have a party.

Linda knew of a secluded lake where they could go and have their own party alone. No one was to bother them or watch them or so they thought.

Three

Linda was up early Monday morning. She made sure her uniform was pressed and everything looked proper.

Today she was going to be introduced to the precinct at roll call.

The shift commander came into the room amongst all the talking and carrying on. One word from him and everything got real still.

"Listen up." He said.

"Today we have a few new people that have reported from the academy and this is their first day on the job. I want all of you to make sure that you get to know them and help them in any way you can."

Linda was so nervous. When her name was called and for her to stand up she looked at the shift commander and noticed he was staring at her.

When roll call was over and the shift was excused to go to work Linda was called out by the commander.

"I haven't had a chance to study your file therefore I'm going to wait before I select your partner for you." He said.

"That's okay, what do you want me to do in the mean time?" she asked him.

"Just stay close to the precinct and help out where you can until I get back with you."

The following Monday the shift commander at roll call announced the she would be with Officer Walker.

They didn't hit it off very good to start with and it got even worse.

Officer Walker wouldn't let Officer Gomez drive nor issue tickets. He kept saying. "Just follow me."

Officer Walker made a few passes towards Officer Gomez in the weeks they worked together and she had to keep her guard up while with him. Once he grabs her butt but said it was an accident before she could say anything.

She told herself she was going to put in for a different partner. She didn't want to start any trouble being a new cop and all.

Four

Today is just an ordinary day for some people. Some were out mowing lawns, kids playing with the garden hoses and others just sitting on their front porches. Having the day off was a day of relaxation and doing regular chores.

There had long hours and less time at the precinct. For Lieutenant Jonathan Wolfgang Wilhelm this is an unusual day off. He worked in homicide at the Cicero One O Five precinct.

Cicero being a suburb of Chicago and some of the most famous from the 20's and 30's by known mobsters such as Al Capone, Machine Gun Kelly, Baby Face Nelson and others during the prohibition days.

No cars in the night with machine guns or blowing up flower shops where mobsters hung out. Now drugs ruled the city and dealers not caring what age got them. Preteens, young boys and girls in elementary school and all the way up, get them hooked and keep them hooked was their motto.

There were other crimes of passion and guilt, murder and mayhem.

The threats of riots were always present when the publics out cries went unanswered. For the One Oh Five precinct and Lieutenant Wilhelm this is a day to enjoy. Not knowing the crimes that were being plotted and carried out was going to be a test for Lieutenant Wilhelm.

For now though he would enjoy himself and use this day as he pleased. Doing what he enjoyed and liked best.

It is a hot day off today. The temperature in the high 90's and he's going to use this Saturday off. Taking a cruise in his Corvette and leaving behind Cicero and getting on Inter-State 55 and heading south. I just might go all the way to Joliet and back. I've taken the t-tops off and I've gassed up the black 1977 Corvette. I am ready to forget everything . . . well almost everything.

Driving the Corvette is relaxing and a lot of fun. The breeze is warm hot coming in the car. Opening up the Corvette and running fast is a joy. That is if a state trooper doesn't pull me over.

I have enough years in the Cicero Homicide Division to retire. Every time I take a ride I always think about retiring and getting into some other line of work. I am up for promotion to captain and if that were to come about.

I would have to serve an extra couple of years to build up enough extra time within the grade. At least I would be behind best to stick around and enjoy a desk for that amount of time. So, maybe it would be the pay increase.

This last case that was finally closed was a trying none on everybody and time consuming.

I have my beeper on but I hope it doesn't go off today.

That's all I need.

Heading south from Cicero doesn't have much scenery some farm land. Not until you pass State road eighty-three do you start seeing open country.

There's something about driving a corvette that makes it special.

Every time an owner of a corvette passes another they always wave. Makes you feel special in a way. Today there are a lot of them out. New and old and it seems I'm the only one alone. The others have a pretty lady beside them and their hair is blowing around their faces and laughing.

Oh, well, I still enjoy my ride and it's getting close to lunch. Maybe I'll Find a drive-in and get me a cheese burger, fries and a Dr Pepper.

As he turned into the drive-in Lieutenant Wilhelm jumped and almost lost control of the car. It was his beeper going off.

It was on vibrate as well as having a beeper sound.

"Man!" I said. It was loud enough for the people coming out of the drive-in to hear. It almost scared me to me to death.

Knowing what it had to be he pulled into a parking spot and went to a pay phone and dialed the number.

Five

It's the precinct I work out of. The detectives in homicide take turns in whatever comes up. Not me, I answer them all and assist when I can.

So much for my day off might as well get it over with and call in.

"Hey Donna, What sup?"

Donna has been with the precinct for years and enjoys being the dispatcher. Her husband died two years ago of cancer. She has had to raise three children by herself.

"Wolf, they need you at the West Riverside street number twelve."

Why my mother gave me a middle name of Wolfgang I'll never know. Wolf has stuck with me since grade school and I have taken the good with the bad with a name like that.

My mother is of German heritage so I guess she thinks

I have to carry some of that along with me in Wolfgang.

"Can you give me any specifics Donna?"

"All I can tell you over the phone is you're not going to like it."

Sure enough, when I arrived there were a lot of squad cars out in front of the house.

Something isn't right about this I told myself and the hair on the back of my neck felt like it was raising up.

There were several ambulances with their lights on and EMT's running towards the house.

Getting out of my Corvette is more work than getting in and at my age it's hard on the joints.

As I am walking up to the small house or apartment as they called it, I see a police officer. He is standing in front of the home. He is a big officer, must be six-three and 240 pounds.

I read Walker on his name tag.

So I say, "What's going down?" all I hear as I pass by is a whisper from him.

"The fucking Wolf comes a sniffing."

"Whoa, just a minute officer," I said as I turned to get in his face.

"Just what do you mean by that remark?"

Walker looks me in the eye and just stares at me.

"Do I know you Officer Walker and do you have a problem with me?" I asked him.

He looked at me and said. "No problem Lieutenant."

As I went by him into the crime scene I sensed his eyes following me.

"I am in the bedroom," I heard one of the detectives call out to me.

It's Detective 2nd grade Jeri Thomas, one of the best in my opinion.

"A female police officer has been murdered and her throat has been cut," she said as she looked up.

"Do you have an ID on her detective Thomas?"

"Yeah, her name is Linda Gomez," she said now looking around in the bedroom. "The crime scene unit has just arrived and they are now starting to process the scene, Lieutenant."

"How about the Medical Examiner, she arrive yet?"

The Medical Examiner is Dr. Dolores Hagan and she is the best. She must have been told there was an officer down to come out tonight and do the processing herself.

"Dr. Hagan, let me know when I can view the crime scene, would you?" I called out to her.

"Wolf, what brings you out here this time of evening?"

"Well doctor, it isn't all that late. Suns just going down and I want to view the scene before it gets cold. I'm going outside to look around Dr. Hagan. If you need me just call out or send someone to find me."

As I made my way out Detective Thomas was standing near the front door.

"Why are you here Detective Thomas?" I asked her.

"I don't live very far from here and I thought maybe if I got here quickly maybe I could help on the case."

"Quickly," I said.

"Yes quickly."

Detective Jeri Thomas has been on the force now probably ten years and a detective for just a few. She is good and thorough in her investigations. Although she doesn't go out on her own she is an asset to whomever she's with.

Detective Thomas is about five feet four and is thin in build. She's has long blond hair and she keeps it up in a ponytail while she's working. She has green eyes, I think, and works out all the time. Ever since her husband was killed in the line of duty a couple of years ago she has maintained a level of physical training bar none to others. She is a black belt in karate and is an expert in firearms as well. She worked and got a degree in criminal justice.

As for me I'm six foot two and 225 pounds. My hair is always kept short. Use to be a flat top years ago but that style has long gone out now. I have thirty years with the department and a lieutenant the last eight years.

"Detective Thomas, will you come outside with me for awhile?" I asked.

"Sure what do you need?"

"I want go over the outside perimeter and thought you might want to accompany me."

"Accompany."

"Yes, accompany," I said and laughed.

I could see that the house was small maybe four rooms and bath.

Outside there were shrubs and flowers near the front entry. The rear was open land with just a small cherry tree. The east side of the house was within about eight feet of the next house. The west side had enough room for a driveway and a small garage in the back.

As we came around the back we could see the back door was standing open and we could see inside.

I called to the crime scene unit to make sure they swept for prints on the back door handles.

"What do you think Detective Thomas?" I asked her.

"It looks like someone used the back door and till we get any prints it could very well be the back door."

"Yeah, that's what I surmised. Front entry not likely unless she knew her assailant and let him in the front door," I said.

"Surmised?" she said.

"Yes, surmised," and we both laughed.

"Okay, Wolf you can come in now," the ME called out.

The two of us went back the same way we came so not to contaminate the crime scene.

As we walked around the house I saw Officer Walker standing down by one of the squad cars talking to another Officer and both of them were looking at me.

"Detective Thomas, is it okay to refer to you by your last name? I know it's not proper to call each other by first name when in company of other police officers or when in the eyes of the public."

"Yeah, sure, call me Thomas if I can call you Wolf."

"Okay, Thomas, what do you know about Officer Walker?" Officer Walker is or was the partner of Linda Gomez.

"Kind of a mutt and Jeff with the size difference of those two," I said.

"Yeah, they took a lot of ribbing," she said. "I don't think Walker was too thrilled about it to be Gomez's partner though." she remarked.

"Why?"

"Well for one thing Gomez was thought to be gay and Officer Walker is very much anti-gay and makes everyone know it."

"So, Thomas any ill feelings between Walker and Gomez you know of?"

"No, they pretty much did their jobs but kept to themselves."

"Come over with me Thomas. I might need a witness."

"You need a witness, Wolf?"

"Yeah," I said. "I don't have a very good feeling about this.

"Wolf sensing an enemy?"

"I'm not sure."

As we walked over to the squad cars Walker and the other fellow police officer broke up. The other one walked away and started for his car.

I whispered to Thomas to get the other officers name.

"Officer Walker, can I talk to you for a minute?"

Officer Walker turned and walked towards me.

"I'm sorry for the comment I made earlier," he said.

"That's okay," although I knew he didn't mean it.

"I hear you were Officer Gomez's partner."

"That's right," he replied as he stared at me.

"I know it must be difficult for you at this time to answer any questions so maybe tomorrow we could get together and go over them."

"Whenever," he said and walked away.

Just then Detective Thomas walked up to me and said, "The other Officers name is Johnson."

I thought this might be a real problem.

"Do you want to be my partner on this case Thomas?"

"You really mean it?"

"Yes, I think it will be needed to have two heads on this one. I plan on doing the investigation myself."

"Working with the Wolf, what more could one asked for."

"Let's try and solve this case and put the bad guys away for good."

"I'm with you if it's okay with my supervisor and yours as well."

"Let's continue to look around some more and talk with the ME and then I'll drive back to the precinct and talk with the Captain."

Six

As I made my way up to the house I was trying to think of a few things that didn't make sense.

Going into the bedroom I looked over and saw Gomez laying across the bed with her head lying on the edge. There was a lot of blood and the smell was terrible. Her throat had been cut from ear to ear and was opened to a terrible gash.

Her hair was long but now matted with her blood. There were some bruises on her arm and neck. The bruises were black and blue so they had to have been put there before she was cut.

The bedroom itself was about a twelve by twelve with a closet to one side.

Gomez wasn't wearing much. Her silk panties were down around her knees and a small gold necklace with a cross on it hanging down from her neck. She was completely naked. She had nice round breasts, no implants.

I asked the CSU tech if he had anything as far as prints were concerned. He told me he dusted everything possible in the bedroom.

I reminded him to get the door knobs and anything else in the kitchen and back porch.

As I was leaving the scene and walked down the front steps I looked up in time to see Walker and Johnson moving in different directions now towards their cars.

I called out to Officer Johnson but he was already in his car and driving away.

I got in my car and went back to my place and fixed me a sandwich and got a cold Dr Pepper out of the fridge. I turned on the TV and watched the Cubs playing the Padres.

Seven

I had a hard time sleeping with the thought of Walker and Johnson on my mind. Something wasn't right and I planned on finding out what it was.

Five-thirty in the morning came awfully fast. I don't think I had more than a couple of hours sleep.

After taking a shower and getting dressed I put on a pot of coffee and ate some sugar smacks cereal.

I packed my gym bag and headed for the gym for a light work out. Early morning is the best time to workout. All the machines and weights are open.

I hit the punching bag for fifteen minutes, jumped rope for five minutes and lifted weights for another ten.

After showering and getting dressed I headed for the precinct.

A. W. Hopkins

Detective Thomas was already there and had brought donuts for the guys. I went over to the coffee mess and poured me a cup of coffee and grabbed a couple of donuts.

I knew better than to wait on getting a donut, especially with these chow hounds around.

Detective Thomas came into my office and sat in one of the two chairs across from my desk.

My office is not very big. There was enough for a desk, two chairs and a filing cabinet.

"How come there are no pictures of the wife and kids on your desk?" Det. Thomas said looking around.

"Well, for one reason there are no kids and I'm not married that answer your question."

"Oh," she replied.

"I have to see the captain in a few minutes and bring him up to speed on the Gomez case so you might as well wait until I'm through."

"Do you still want me to assist you on this case?" she said.

"Yes, I haven't changed my mind."

I could see a worried look on her face when she asked me with a frown.

I told her to wait until I got back and we would go over our notes.

Eight

Believe it or not our Captain's name is John C. Penny or as we call him Captain J.C. Penny. He hates that, so we call him J.C. Penny all the more.

The Captains office is bigger than mine. He can get four chairs, two filing cabinets and a bigger desk in his office than mine. He has two windows looking out to the other desks and pictures of family on his desk. A lot of wall plaques naming him Mr. this and that.

Captain Penny is about five-ten and his weight is about two twenty-five. He keeps his head shaved so there's no telling how much hair he would really have if left to grow out. He's black and will go the extra mile for any of his detectives that need him.

Today he has on a black suit, white shirt that fits him tight a round the stomach and a red tie on. He always wears his black wing tipped shoes. The suit coat is off now really showing the shirt stretching around him. He's also eating a powdered donut and as he looks up at me he's got white powder all around his mouth.

As I enter his office he motions for me to sit down wiping the powder off his face.

"Have a seat Wolf and tell me about Officer Gomez."

"Someone cut her throat Captain and left no clues to speak of."

I didn't know if I should mention Walker yet or not.

I really had nothing on him so bringing him up would only cause trouble for me, so I kept quite.

"Someone said she was gay captain. A lesbian but I haven't had time to check that out for sure."

"Ah, Christ, do you think that had anything to do with the killing?" Cap asked me.

"Don't know yet but I'll let you know as soon as I find out anything."

"Well do the best you can and keep me posted."

"Captain Penney I'm going to take this case if it's alright with you. One of our own went down and I feel I should pursue this."

"It's okay with me Wolf. Do you need any help on the case?"

"Cap, I would like to have Detective 2nd grade Jeri Thomas, to assist me if you don't mind."

"Isn't she the one that her husband was killed in the line of duty a few years ago?" Cap asked me.

"I believe so and I think she will make a good detective.

She was on the scene when I got there yesterday evening and requested to assist on the case."

"Okay, I'll get the necessary paperwork made out and assign her on the case as the second person with you and talk to her supervisor."

"I'm going to need Gomez's file and I'm going to talk to her partner Officer Walker also."

"Why, her partner?"

"Well, he was on the scene and I wonder why." I replied.

"There are a few questions I need to ask."

I went back to my officer and Detective Thomas had looked over my notes and was sitting and going over her notes now when I entered.

"Detective Thomas, it looks like you're stuck with me for a while."

"Really," she said jumping up and dropping her notes on the floor.

"Yep, captain is getting the paperwork started assigning you to me."

"What's first," she said rubbing her hands together.

"I want Officer Walker brought in. Then we can really start getting a feel for this case." I told her picking up the papers she dropped and putting them back in the folder.

"What do you think of Officer Walker?"

"Need to start some place and he's as good a place to start."

"Amen to that," she said putting her folder away.

Nine

I had Officer Walker called into my officer at one in the afternoon. Detective Thomas and I were present in my office when he came in. Walker looked bigger now than he did yesterday. He didn't have his cap on this time and I could see that he had shaved his head. It was shining from the over head lights.

"You requested to see me Lieutenant?" He said as he entered my office.

"Yes I did."

"What do you want me for?" He was looking over towards Detective Thomas.

"I have few questions is all for right now," I said looking at him. "One question comes to mind as to what you were doing there last evening?"

Walker looked at me and said. "We were partners."

"Yes I know that but why then?"

"I went over to pick up Gomez to start our shift," he said.

"I always pick her up."

"So, when you got there what did you do?" I was curious and was looking at his facial expressions.

"When I rang the door bell and she didn't answer I went around to the back door and found it open."

"What then?" I asked leaning back in my chair.

"I pushed the door the rest of the way open with my elbow as not to leave any fingerprints on it. I called out to her but she didn't answer."

"And then," trying to keep the conversation going.

"When she didn't respond I drew my weapon and went in with caution."

"Did you call for back up Officer Walker?" I asked as Detective Thomas was looking on.

"I found the house to be empty and Officer Gomez's body on the bed. Her throat had been cut."

"Then what did you do?"

"I called the EMT's and the Crime Scene Unit, Also the medical examiner's office."

"Officer Walker did you like Officer Gomez?"

"She was my partner."

"That's not what I asked you," I said. "Is it true what they say about her being gay?"

"I don't know what you're trying to imply here, Lieutenant."

"Well, Gomez was a very attractive woman and you're her partner, right?"

"Look, she was my partner that's all so let it be."

"Did you ever try to come on to her being a big guy like you are and be rejected?" I said.

"No," he said and looked straight into my eyes and stared.

I stared back at him and after awhile I let him go back to his duty section.

"You sure stirred him up didn't you?" Det. Thomas said.

"I wanted to see how he would react to a question like that."

"Well you got the reaction that's for sure. In fact if looks could kill you would be dead Wolf."

"I know."

Detective Thomas and I were getting thirsty and hungry so we decided to go out and get a bite to eat. As we walked out of the precinct I could see Officer Walker getting into his squad car and pull away. He was busy looking at me and almost hit another patrol car coming into the lot.

We got into my unmarked police car, a Buick, not fast but comfortable to ride in. I turned the air conditioner on right a way. Ninety plus degrees is way to hot for anybody, especially one wearing a tie like me. I loosened my tie.

Ten

Detective Thomas and I went back to the crime scene and checked the neighborhood to see if we could find any clues.

The neighbor next door was a small thin male, looked and talked like Barney Fife. He didn't want any trouble so I went to the house on the other side of Gomez's house.

When I rang the door bell I could see the blinds move so I decided to stay until someone answered the door. After waiting about five minutes of ringing the door bell someone finally opened the door. This time a woman answered the door.

"Hello, we are here to ask you a few more questions since last night if you don't mind?" I said.

"Are you the police?"

"Yes, and I'm Lieutenant Wilhelm and this is my partner. We showed her our ID and she invited us inside.

The woman was in her forties I would guess. Body was of big bone but not fat. She wore her hair tied up in the back and no make up on.

"Can I get the two of you something to drink, coffee or a soda?"

"No thanks," We both replied.

"What can I do to help the police?"

"We're trying to find someone that might be able to help us in finding someone that knows Officer Gomez."

"If you know anything at all that would help please tell us now." Det. Thomas asked.

"Did you see anything that might help, such as a car or persons visiting in and out?" I asked her.

"Any boyfriends, girl friends, you know, someone she might have hung around with off duty?" Thomas asked.

"Well, there was one female friend that came over a lot.

I think her name was Beverly something."

"By the way for the record could we have your name so we can establish this interview?" Thomas asked.

"I'm so sorry for not introducing myself. My name is Dottie."

"Okay Dottie, about Beverly, do you know anything about her. What she looks like, the car she drives anything at all."
I said.

"I don't know her last name but she is tall, thin and has real short black hair. Sort of a Hispanic look you know," she said.

"What make of car did she drive?"

"I think it was an older car. I think it was a fire bird maybe. It had a big bird on the hood and the car was red. Made a lot of noise as if the muffler was coming off," she said rubbing her hands together.

"How often did she come to visit Linda Gomez?" Thomas asked.

"She visited most of the weekends if Linda didn't work and stayed the whole weekend. That's about all I know to tell you right now."

I took one of my cards and handed it to her.

"If you think of anything else let me know. Call me there where you can reach me."

"Well, now all we have to do is find this Beverly and we will be all set," said Thomas.

"It might not be all that tough."

"Oh, and what makes you so sure?"

"We'll go to the funeral and watch the guest list and see who attends. Let's call it a day and come back tomorrow fresh and ready to go." I said to Thomas.

"Lieutenant is it okay if I ask you something?"

"Sure what is it?"

"Could we refer to each other in private as maybe just Jeri and Wolf?"

"Okay Jeri, you can but remember not in public. I don't want it getting back to the Captain and getting you in trouble."

"Getting me in trouble, what about you?"

"Look Jeri, I've been around longer than you and I can handle something like this but you don't need it on your record, Okay?"

"Okay."

"I'll drop you off back at the station so you can get your car."

"That's fine. What are you going to do?"

A. W. Hopkins

"I think I'm going to the Dew Drop In and have a few beers."
After dropping Jeri off I could see she was driving an older car.
It was a few years old anyway. It still looked nice though.

Eleven

I called Dr. Hagan on her cell phone and she told me she was at Mac Neal Hospital in the basement in the morgue.

That's where the autopsy was being held.

I called Jeri and told her to meet me at the hospital parking lot at 9 a.m. tomorrow morning.

I was in my car waiting maybe ten minutes past 9 when she drove up and parked beside me. I could see she had her hair done up in a ponytail so I knew she was ready to go to work.

I got out of the Buick which I drive five days a week. Jeri out of her car and we both walked to the front door.

"Good morning Jeri,"

"Good morning to you to."

She asked me. "Is this autopsy going to be bad or what?"

"Have you ever been in on an autopsy before, Detective?"

"No way Jose," she said.

"Well the first one is always the one you will always remember. You don't have to go in if you don't want to Detective Thomas."

"No I want to."

When we entered the lobby I went over to the information booth and told them where we were going. I came back and looked at Detective Thomas.

"We have to take the elevator to the basement then walk to our left two doors down to the ME's office," I said.

"Swell, I'll just follow you," she replied.

"Swell," and laughed.

Dr. Hagan was in her officer and she looked up and saw us as we entered.

"Wolf," she yelled and came around her desk and gave him a hug. "Except for last night long time no see."

"Doctor Hagan this is Detective Jeri Thomas and she is assisting on this case." I said.

"Lucky you Jeri," Doctor Hagan replied.

"Now you need to get a gown on both of you. Put slippers on over your shoes and the masks are in the changing room."

We went into different changing rooms and changed.

As we walked towards the autopsy room I spied a jar of Vicks and opened it and took some with my fingers and put it under my nose. I offered Jeri some but she waved her head no. Must be trying to be macho or just doesn't know any better.

We walked through the door and I put my mask on. I looked around and saw Jeri turning and holding her nose trying to go back out the door. She was grabbing for the Vicks jar and I started laughing.

When she came back in she looked at me and saw I was laughing.

"You could have told me what the Vicks was for," she said.

"Sorry," I said.

"Sorry my ass, you wanted a laugh and you got it."

"Okay Detective Thomas you're right and I apologize."

"Thanks."

The room was a pale blue color and two empty gurneys up against the far wall. We could see the big cooler they kept the ones to be autopsied in.

There was a table with various instruments and a saw on it next to Dr. Hagan. The assistant was in his garments and had a paper mask on as well.

Dr. Hagan had Officer Gomez's body on the table but the sheet was still over her. The only thing showing was the name tag hanging from her right big toe.

Thomas and I moved on the opposite side from Dr. Hagan on the other side of the table.

The sheet was removed by the doctor and as Linda Gomez's body became visible it was a bluish gray looking.

The blood had been wiped clean. The cut below her chin was open and looked really deep. Almost like the person tried to cut her head off.

I looked over at Jeri and she didn't look to well.

Dr. Hagan said. "It looks like she was cut from left to right and the killer was behind her when it happened."

"So doctor, are you saying the person was right handed that did this?" I asked looking down at the body.

"Yes, because to inflict such a cut the body had to be steadied while the cut was made."

"What about the bruises on her?" Jeri asked.

"It looks to me like she had been held for a while, before being killed."

"Can you give me an up date on her tests when you get around to it and if there were any drugs, and the time of death?"

Dr. Hagan reached over and grabbed the chest cavity saw and started it up. That was all for Jeri. She turned and ran out of the autopsy room with her hand over her nose and mouth.

"Poor girl, I feel sorry for her," Dr. Hagan said.

"Yeah, her first autopsy," I said.

Twelve

I asked Detective Thomas if she was hungry after we left.

"If you want to clean this car up after I eat. It's okay with me. Right now is not a good time for my stomach."

We agreed that she should at least get something to drink.

"We can pull in at a drive thru and get you a 7up and me a Dr Pepper."

"Okay."

"After the body has been released to the family I want to talk to them," I said to Jeri.

"You think they know who this Beverly is?"

"I don't know but it's a try."

"What now Wolf?"

We pulled in to the drive thru and ordered our drinks and I said. "We'll check our folders again."

We left the drive thru and after a few pulls on the straw I looked over towards her and her color was starting to come back.

"7up sure does help a squeamish stomach."

I told her I wanted to check with the lab and find out what we could about the fingerprints if any.

"Is there something you're looking for that I'm not aware of?" Jeri asked looking at me.

"I'd rather not say anything just yet." I need to wait a while.

"Okay."

"Do we know anything about Walker and Johnson, Jeri?"

"No, in fact don't you think we should pull both of their folders and look?"

"Jeri, let's go back to the station and see what we can find out."

"Sure why not." She replied. "Why do you refer to the precinct as the station?"

"I don't know, maybe from habit listening to the older cops referring to it being the station."

"I was just wondering."

We had the some free time this afternoon so I asked Jeri if she wanted to go to the firing range for awhile.

"I'm with you, remember."

Thirteen

I drove us out to the firing range and we both had to sign in and collected our ammunition and went to the middle two booths.

I took out my Glock 9 mm and checked the ammo all ready in the magazine as did Jeri. She had a Glock 9 also.

"You want to go first Jeri or me?"

"Go ahead Lieutenant and remember where we're at."

"Oops forgot."

"We'll start at thirty yards and work back to forty, okay detective Thomas?"

"No problem Wolf, eh, I mean Lieutenant."

"Okay, ear muffs on and safety glasses on," I said looking down at my weapon.

I fired five rounds at twenty yards and hit the bulls-eye four times and the fifth just outside the ring. As I started to say something

Detective Thomas pulled on my shirt sleeve and motioned with her head back towards the entrance

Officer Walker and Johnson were just coming thru the door when I was looking at my target. Walker looked at it and laughed.

"Looks like the Wolf isn't as good as everyone thought," Walker said to me with a smirk.

"Don't have to be good most times, lucky will do," I said looking at him.

"I thought you were better than that though."

"You know Walker if I didn't know better, I would think you're trying to goad me into a shooters match."

"Now, what makes you think that Wolf. I can shoot better than you any day."

"Tell you what I'll do Officer Walker. I'll put Detective Thomas up against you and a side bet of fifty bucks."

I could feel Detective Thomas pulling on the back of my shirt in fact tugging is more like it.

Walker looked at Johnson and he nodded his head. He thought this was going to be easy money for him.

"Okay Wolf, You call it."

"Ten rounds, five at thirty yards and then five at forty yards. Five rounds first by one then the other then the other shooter. Second five rounds you'll switch places. Okay?"

"Okay, flip a coin and see who goes first. We'll let the little Detective call it." He said.

I flipped the coin in the air and detective Thomas called heads.

I caught the coin flipped it on the back of my hand and pulled my other hand away.

"Heads it is," Every one said.

"Your call Detective," Walker said smirking.

"She wants to go first," I said.

"But . . . But . . . But," she said.

"No buts about it, okay?" I said looking at her.

Detective Thomas put a new target on the pulley and ran it down to thirty yards. She put her ear muffs on and safety glasses. We all did the same. She assumed the proper stance and took a deep breath and let it out and fired five rounds at the target. Finished she pulled the target up and she had five rounds in the bulls-eye.

"Seems the little detective got lucky," Walker said looking over at Johnson.

I looked at Walker and said. "It's your turn."

Walker then ran his target down and assumed the proper stance grip. He fired five rounds and pulled up the target.

Five rounds in the bulls-eye.

"Looks like the pressures on the little detective," He said smiling.

Man, I could see the anger in her eyes when he called her a little detective.

"You first this time Walker." I said.

Walker ran his target down to forty yards and assumed the stance and fired five rounds. When he was finished he pulled his target up. Four rounds in the bulls-eye and the fifth was just outside by a whisker.

"Beat that." He said.

Detective Thomas looked at me and I whispered in her ear.

"Kick ass little detective."

Little detective my ass, she mumbled.

Thomas after assuming the proper stance took a deep breath and fired five rounds.

When the target came up I looked over at Walker and the smirk was gone. It was replaced by a redness and anger.

"Well well," I said. "Looking here, looks like I made an easy fifty bucks Officer Walker. Five are in the bulls-eye."

He took out his wallet and placed two twenties and a ten down and left.

I heard him tell Johnson to shut up on the way out.

"Why did you do that Lieutenant? Putting me up against Walker."

"Detective Thomas there's times in life you have to take charge and let the other people know you're not going to be trampled on."

"That's what this was about,"

"Yes detective it was and you passed."

"Thanks."

We gave each other a high five and she finally started laughing.

"You know detective I probably could make a hundred bucks on you taking Walker on in the ring."

"Don't even think it Wolf. So help me if you do."

I looked at her and we both started Laughing.

"I did kick ass didn't I?"

"Yes, for a little detective you did."

"Don't even go there, Okay."

"Okay."

We finally left and returned to the precinct and filed our reports for the day.

Fourteen

Officer Gomez's body was released to the family after the autopsy for the funeral arrangements and burial. The police department refused to have a proper police funeral for her sighting that she wasn't in the line of duty when she was killed. I have seen other Officers not in the line of duty receive a public police funeral. I wonder if being gay had any thing to do with it and the public knowing of the circumstances of her death.

At the grave site there were a lot of police officers attending but none in uniform that I could see.

Both Thomas and I finally had our eye on Beverly Sutton or at least that's what the guest book had in it at the funeral home.

As the funeral started breaking up I told Jeri to check Beverly out and get her address or telephone number from her so we could talk later. I told her I was going to approach the mom and dad and find out what I could. I started over to them hoping to talk before they got in the limo and drove a way.

"Could I have a word with you two before you leave?"

I said as I walked up to them.

I had my ID out and showed it to them and introduced myself.

The mother was still crying yet when I looked over at the father I could see that he had never shed a tear for his dead daughter.

Dad looked at me and said. "We have nothing to say."

"Don't you want justice to be served and the guilty person or persons brought in?"

"I think justice has been already served," He replied.

"Henry, that's not fair and you know it," the mother said looking at her husband.

"I have one question to ask and I know this may not be the time but it has to be answered sooner or later. Was Linda gay?"

"Go to hell!" Dad replied and they got into the limo and drove off.

Jeri was walking towards me when I turned around and looked at her.

"I've got both address and phone number from Beverly," she said.

"At least you did better than me," and I told her about my conversation with Linda's parents.

"Henry, why did you treat the lieutenant that way? You know he had no knowledge of Linda's past."

"Harriet, I don't want to talk about this. Linda was our baby and look what she became. She became a lesbian that's what."

"Henry, that's enough. Linda couldn't help what she be came no more than what we are."

"Bull shit Harriet, we had no part in making her the way she was and you know it."

Henry and Harriet rode the rest of the way back to the funeral home in silence.

"I'm not going to talk about this any more Henry and you better not either." Harriet thinking of her baby girl left behind and knowing they'd probably never be back to put flowers on her grave again Henry was left with only thoughts of her daughter and why things were what they were.

Fifteen

Dr. Hagan called my beeper while I was eating a sandwich and washing it down with a Dr Pepper. I had just stopped for a bite to eat before going back to work from a workout at the gym. Working out at lunch time is tough because so many guys and females try to get a quick work out also. After looking at my beeper I dialed Dr. Hagan's office on my cell phone.

"Okay doctor what have you got for me?"

"Wolf, the toxicology results are back and Linda Gomez had quite a bit of Xanax and alcohol in her blood."

"So what does that tell me? Someone spiked her drink and then killed her," I asked.

"Enough Xanax and alcohol will render a person unconscious and useless."

"Did she have already had the pills and alcohol in her stomach? Then be unconscious when the killer came in?"

I asked her.

"You mean attempted suicide, Wolf?"

"Doc, she was unhappy and scared of her partner and had already been denied a request for transfer,"

"Whoever did this was close to her and wanted her in a stupor."

"I appreciate your call and how long before we get the DNA results back?"

"There's not enough evidence to submit for DNA Wolf." She said.

"You mean doctor that the person that killed Linda Gomez didn't leave any trace of DNA?"

"Nope . . . and another thing Linda Gomez was raped before she was killed."

"You mean that Linda Gomez, a lesbian, was raped before she was killed."

"You got it Wolf and he used a condom."

"Any trace of it?" I knew that was a dumb question but you have ask the question.

"Those bruises were from someone holding her down while raping her then cut her. Wolf I think the rape was to make a point."

"Thanks doc."

"No problem, just catch those bastards. Okay?"

I called Detective Thomas and told her what I found out from Dr. Hagan and told her to meet me in my office in ten minutes.

I took out a note pad and started writing as many note as I could up to this point.

Sixteen

This was a hate crime and we had to start looking at friends and even her partner.

"Where do you want us to start?" Jeri looked over at me and I could see concern on her face.

"Let's go and see Beverly Sutton and maybe she can shed some light on her friend."

Beverly Sutton lived on the east side of Chicago and in a run down apartment complex. Buildings all around with windows broke out and kids running around with hardly anything on in this heat. A gang was hanging out in an empty lot where there use to be a basketball court. The basketball ring was bent straight down and weeds growing all around. Her apartment was on the third floor.

We finally arrived after walking around junk and homeless people living in the halls. The elevator was broken and the stairs . . .

well, something else. The stairwell smelled of urine, pot and alcohol. It kind of made you sick and high at the same time.

We called ahead so that she would be aware of us coming. I hoped her apartment would look better inside then what it looked like outside all around.

Beverly answered the door and I could see she took time to fix herself up.

She was close to five-ten and about 130 pounds, long black hair with makeup on. She was a very beautiful woman.

She let us in and asked if we wanted ice tea to drink, I had to have sweet and low for mine and Detective Thomas took hers plain, unsweetened.

Her apartment was plain no expensive furniture, in fact the couch had a few rips here and there. It looked like the chair had a spring ready to come through the cushion. There was one end table by the couch. The kitchen you could see from the living room and the linoleum on the kitchen floor was cracked and coming up. A small nineteen inch TV sat in one corner of the living room on a small stand.

We introduced ourselves and asked if it would okay to tape our conversation. Beverly said it would be okay. So I got the tape recorder out of my pocket, turned it on and laid it down in front of me.

"Beverly," I started the conversation, "How long have you known Linda Gomez?"

"Linda and I have been friends even before she started with the police and going to the academy."

"Beverly, did you know Linda was gay?" Thomas asked.

"Yes, she and I are gay or she was."

"Did she have any one that might have wanted to hurt her or kill her that you know of?" I asked while taking a sip of my tea.

"Did Officer Walker, her partner give her any trouble or cause any problems for her?" Thomas asked looking at me.

"Linda said that Walker was a skin head and hated gays and she had to be careful around him," Beverly said looking up at the ceiling.

"What do you mean by that? That she acted as if she was straight around him." I asked her.

"She just said that she had to be careful and that she wished she could get a different partner."

Thomas asked. "She put in for a transfer request for a different partner, didn't she?"

"Yes, she told me that she thought someone higher up put her with Walker on purpose. Someone that knew she was gay and wanted them together."

"How did someone else happen to find it out? Then we have to think Walker knew all along . . . right?" I asked.

Detective Thomas and I looked at each other with a puzzled look.

"You're saying Beverly that Linda was placed as Officer Walker's partner knowing that someone knew she was gay and Walker hated gays?" I said looking at her.

"That's what she told me."

"What about when she was at the Police Academy? Did she go in as a gay person or what?" Det. Thomas asked.

"No, Linda and a few other gay friends went in together and had a little group made up amongst themselves. They posed as straight people and only dated each other, you know, guy and gal."

"They kept their homosexuality a secret."

"What about this group that you are speaking of. How many how there?"

Thomas asked.

"I believe there were four of them."

"You mean two of each, guys and women?" I asked.

"I believe Linda said there were, plus one more guy."

"They got together and took the tests and then the physicals and passed. During the Academy they worked together and stuck together so no one would find out."

"What happen at graduation?"

"They were separated and sent to different precincts here in Chicago."

I asked. "Do you know the names of the other four cadets that Linda Gomez had gone through the Academy with?"

Beverly looked at me and started to say something then turned her head. I could sense she was holding back tears.

"What? "I said.

"Nothing," She said wiping her eyes with a napkin.

"Come on Beverly, help us out. If you know anything let us know," Thomas said.

"It's just that I don't want what to say."

"Are you scared Beverly? Has someone talked to you?"

I said looking at her as she looked down and away from me.

"No."

"Talk to us Beverly so we can find the killer," Thomas said.

"Linda said one of the guys in their group applied for a position out in San Francisco and his application was accepted and then transferred."

"Linda said she thought there was a group that was called "The Blue Society." They're a vigilante group within the police force," Beverly said looking at me with tears in her eyes.

I said. "Beverly, please help us, Okay?"

Thomas asked. "Did Linda give any names in this group?"

Beverly shook her head no. "Linda told me she heard talk about it in the locker room one day. When they saw her they all quit talking and broke up."

"If you hear anything else or remember anything call us,"

Wolf said as he reached in his pocket and got a card out and handed it to her.

"Remember Beverly anything."

"You know Beverly's apartment wasn't to bad compared to the outside," Thomas spoke up after leaving.

"Yeah, depressing isn't it."

"Yes, depressing."

Seventeen

"What now Wolf?" Det. Thomas said as we walked back to the car.

"I think we need to find out who all was in Linda's class at the academy and go from there."

I thought maybe we could find out more details back at the precinct.

"Maybe we need to talk to someone that had a locker close to hers. Maybe some locker room gossip," I said.

"Sounds like you want me to do a little snooping in the locker room?"

"Snooping?"

"Yeah, snooping," Jeri said. "Okay I'll spend some time in the locker room and see what I can find out."

We both finally buckled up and I started the car and pulled away Jeri looked over at me and said. "Do you have any ideas?"

"I've got a few but playing them out is another thing and I want to be sure of what's going down."

As we pulled into the parking lot and I pulled into my spot a couple officers looked over at us and said some thing to one another. One of them started to laugh and said something back and they both laughed.

When we got out of the car one of the officers came over and looked at Detective Thomas.

He said. "Hey, Detective Thomas, how does it feel to work with the Wolf?"

"Well officer, ah Thompson," looking at his name tag. "It is better to learn from the best than to run with the rest don't you think?"

Officer Thompson just looked at her and then turned and walked away.

"You okay Thomas?"

"'Yeah, I'm okay, I'm sure everyone knows by now about the firing range incident, don't you?"

"Not if Officer Walker has anything to say about it." I said.

When we entered the building Jeri took the stairs to the basement and to the women's locker room. I went on up to my office. Captain Penney was waiting for me and called me into his office.

"Lieutenant Wilhelm what happened out at the pistol range yesterday?" He asked.

"News travels fast, Cap."

"Anything I should be concerned about," He said with a smile on his face.

"Nah, I think Detective Thomas handled everything just find . . . just find."

The Captain shook his head and gave me the thumbs up as I left.

Eighteen

As I was getting ready to leave and go back to my place Detective Thomas came out the door.

"Hey, Detective Thomas over here," I yelled.

She looked over and saw me and waved and came over.

"Find out anything?"

"No, everybody stopped talking when I walked into the locker room."

"It must be tough."

"What must be tough?"

"For women to stop talking," I said laughing.

"Yeah right, what now smarty pants?"

"I'm going home and take a shower and go to the Dew Drop In for a beer."

"See you later then Wolf."

I got into my Buick and headed home to my place and a nice hot shower. After showering and brushing my teeth.

I shaved again and put on some Old Spice after shave. I was dressed in blue jeans, tee shirt and sandals. I went out the door and ready to drive my corvette to the pub.

When I got there the place was just starting to come to life. The bartender brought over my draft beer and some peanuts. The juke box was alive and jumping. ZZ Top was on now playing 'Legs.'

Young women were dancing with no one in particular as their partner. Bump and grind. Some of them I swear could be belly dancers easily. Me, I like a slow dance, you know, rub bellies and belt buckles.

Country and western was playing now on the juke box. I sat in a far corner by myself. There was a small table for two. I had a few women come over and sit and talk small talk but got up and left later on. That was okay with me because I wasn't interested in them either.

The pool tables were busy. Always seems like the biggest crowd was around the pool tables. So I put my quarter on the edge of the table to challenge the winner. I'm not real good but not real bad either. I can beat the average players easily so I tend to stay away from the tables because I don't want anyone to think I'm too good for them. I have lost a few games on purpose because of that. Not tonight through.

About eleven the better players were starting to show up and I was still on the table.

I heard some one whistle and a few cat calls from the crowd but gave it no mind.

I saw an arm reach out and put a quarter on the edge of the table. I was still to busy to look up. After sinking the eight ball I looked up.

When I did there she stood.

"Jeri?"

"Thought I would check out the Dew Drop In," She said.

She had hair down below her shoulders, cut off blue jeans and a tank top on, pink at that. She was wearing sandals with about a one inch heel.

"Want to shoot some pool Jeri?"

"Sure, what's the stakes?"

"This is just for fun that's all," I said looking up around at the guys with their tongues hanging out, "No money here just fun."

"Shucks I thought we were going to play for more than just fun."

"Okay Jeri, how about ten bucks?"

"Flip to see who breaks," she said.

She called heads and shot first. She didn't put any in on the break. I put a striped ball in and missed the second. Every time Jeri leaned over to shoot guys would line up on the opposite side of the table from her just to look down her top. I got where I would line up directly across from her to keep the guys back.

We finally got down to the eight ball and I'm trying my best to beat her. Jeri sank the eight ball and finally beat me.

"What'd you do Wolf let her beat you?" They were saying and laughing at me.

"Don't want to beat the lady?" Another one said.

One skinning dude put his quarter up on the edge of the table and looked at Jeri.

"Come on little lady, I'll beat you."

Oh, oh I said to myself.

"Little lady, looks like you have been challenged," I said.

The skinning dude got the break but that's all. Jeri ran the table and everybody got real quite after that.

"Are you good at everything you do?" I asked her.

"Everything or I don't do it," She said.

"Let's go sit down for awhile Jeri."

"Okay."

I had another beer and Jeri had a vodka and tonic.

"You look very nice tonight Jeri I must say."

"Thanks."

"Are you comfortable with me sitting here with you, Wolf?"

"You are a lot younger than me, though it is nice to have you here."

"Thank you, Wolf?" She looked at me. "You aren't that much older, maybe in your 50's?"

"Yes."

"You weigh what? 240."

"Two Twenty."

"What, about Six-four."

"Six-two and a half," I said.

"You've never been married . . . right?"

"No but close a few times."

"What happened to keep someone like you from going down the aisle?"

"I don't know. Maybe being a cop or not having the right chemistry. Who knows?"

"What about you Jeri?"

"I was married as you know and my husband was killed in the line of duty."

"Yes I heard something about that. Want to talk about it?"

"I don't know. Sometimes I get caught up in it again thinking about it."

"My husband and his partner answered a domestic fight. The woman's husband had a baseball bat and was going to hit her with it when we got there,"

"Domestics are the worst," I said

"Yes they are. My husband started putting the handcuffs on the guy and his wife grabbed a knife from the kitchen and stabbed my husband in the back of the neck. He was in ICU for two days before he died."

I ordered another beer and Jeri had another vodka and tonic. I guess we were getting a little drunk. Jeri asked me to dance but I told her only the slow ones, so she waited for a George Strait song. I could smell her hair. The shampoo she used smelled really good and the perfume she had on was great.

She was shorter compared to me. Coming up to about my arm pits and probably weighing 120 pounds. She had a nice tan and blond hair.

The crowd was really getting loud and the smoke was so thick a person almost needed a knife to cut through it. A few guys got into a fight over another woman and the bartender threw them out.

I asked Jeri how she had gotten here and she said she had a taxi bring her. She didn't want to drink and drive. I wished I had thought of that. I wasn't about to leave my corvette in the parking lot. I asked her if I could give her a lift home since we both had enough to drink for the evening.

After getting in the car and trying to clear my head we both buckled up. I didn't drive fast . . . in fact a little under the speed limit.

When I drove up I said. "Here you go your home."

Jeri looked out. "This isn't my place Wolf."

"Damn," I said. "This is my place. Look Jeri you can stay in the guest room and I'll take you home tomorrow. Okay?"

"Okay."

We both got out and I unlocked the door and we went in. I made sure the guest room was okay to sleep in and told her where the bathroom was and extra towels. I went to my bedroom and closed the door. I got in bed and all I could think of was Jeri out there in the guest room. My door opened and Jeri stuck her head in and said. "Good night Wolf. I had a nice time tonight."

"Me too," I said.

Next morning we both got up with our heads feeling like they would explode.

Jeri showered first while I fixed some bacon and eggs, toast and coffee.

"The coffee smells good," she said.

We ate and drank our coffee then I took a shower and dressed. The bathroom smelled terrific since Jeri was in here before me. One of my tee shirts was lying on the floor where she put it. She must have gotten it out of the dryer to wear to bed in. She had to use my soap but her perfume made my bathroom smell so good.

I drove her home and went over to the gym to workout.

Although my head hurt I still needed the workout. The rest of the weekend went by fast as they always do.

I tried to put my thoughts into order but the more I would think the more out of order they became so I quit thinking. I got a cold Dr Pepper out of the ice box and sat down and watched the NASCAR race.

Nineteen

When I got to the precinct Jeri was already there and talking with the other detectives. I also saw the donuts on the table by the coffee mess.

"Keep bringing in donuts and the homicide division will be listed as the obese division," I said.

"Quit complaining," the guys said.

"Detective Thomas would you come into my office?"

"You want coffee and a donut first?" She said looking at me.

"Later."

Detective Thomas entered my office and shut the door behind her.

"What's the matter, something bothering you?" She said.

"It's about Friday night Jeri and I don't want to get feelings mixed up in this investigation."

"Why, are you having mixed feelings Wolf?"

"No, I thought maybe you had."

"Not me, I had a good time and let it go at that."

"Good, now that's settled let's get started on this case,"
I said.

"Okay."

"We know for a fact this is a hate crime by the manner it happened and the message that has been sent," I told her.

"Do you think it's a message for other cops or for gays?"
Thomas said.

"I think after carefully studying and thinking about what I have heard, it's against gay cops."

Thomas had a concerned look on her face.

"You're thinking about what Beverly Sutton told us aren't you Wolf."

"That's part of it. I can't get Walker out of my mind."

"Me either."

"We need to find out if Walker has an alibi."

"I'm going to make another call to Dr. Hagan and ask a few more questions. I want you to listen in."

As I dialed the Medical Examiner's office a few things started buzzing in my mind.

The phone rang and doctor Hagan picked up the phone.

"Medical Examiner's office," She said.

"Hello, Dr. Hagan."

"Wolf that you?"

"Yes speaking."

"What can I do for you this morning?"

"Can you release any more information to me about what you found during the autopsy?"

"Like what."

"Do you know what kind of knife was used to kill Linda Gomez?"

"I can tell you that it was more than likely a knife with a four inch blade approximately and with a sharp edge." She said.

"Could it be a hunting knife or a pocket knife with a folding blade?"

"It could be a steak knife also," she said.

"Were there any steak knifes present in Gomez's house that fits for the weapon?"

"Did you find any in the examination of the crime scene? Wolf."

"No."

"I believe the killer or killers took the knife with them when they left."

"You mean more than one killer's, doc?"

"Maybe there were, don't rule it out. The killer didn't know of Linda's condition so he very well could have had another person with him. If he had waited she would have died of the over dose saving him a murder charge, but, then again he wanted to make a statement."

"Good point Dr. Hagan. Then if your theory is true then the parties entered from the front and not the back."

"It's possible."

"Thanks doc, talk to you again."

"It's my pleasure."

I hung up the phone and looked at Detective Thomas.

"What do you think?"

"I think the back door was opened to make it look like an entry and exit for the killer as the doctor said," answered Det. Thomas.

"I need to make another call so listen in."

"I'm all ears, Wolf."

"No you're not by a long shot."

"What?"

"All ears."

"Make the call," Thomas said while laughing.

"Hello, whom am I speaking to in the Crime Scene Unit there?"

"This is Amy, what can I do for you?"

"This is Lieutenant Jonathan Wilhelm with the homicide division and I would like to speak to someone there about the fingerprints taken at the Linda Gomez crime scene."

"Hold on and I'll transfer you, Okay?"

I looked at Jeri and she had her fingers crossed.

"What do you need?" A male voice came over the telephone.

"Do you have the results of the fingerprints taken at the apartment?"

"Sure, but they're all cops as far as prints go," he said.

"Did you dust the back door?"

"We sure did."

"Was there any drinking glasses lying around?" I said.

"There were glasses in the sink but they had been washed out and left to dry."

"What did you find out other than that?"

"There wasn't anything else"

"Okay thanks."

Detective Thomas didn't have her fingers crossed any more and looked disappointed.

"So, where are we at now Wolf? What's bothering you?"

"If there is such a society out there that is bent on revenge maybe it is wide spread."

"You mean other precincts and possibly other states as well."

"Send out e-mails to other law enforcements on the net and see if we get any hits and I think it's time to bring in Officer Johnson also," I said.

I made the call to have Officer Johnson meet me in my office after lunch. A little after one Officer Johnson showed up.

He had his uniform all pressed and looked impressive in it. He was tall, thin built. He didn't have his head shaved. He had it in a butch though. He had brown hair, brown eyes. He knocked on the door. I motioned for him to come in.

"Captain called my shift supervisor and requested I report to your office." He said shutting the door behind him.

"Thanks for coming in," I said looking up.

"Why do you want to see me?"

"I have some routine questions. I saw you there at Linda Gomez's apartment so I thought maybe you might be of help to us."

"I responded to the call just like the others did."

"Do you know Officer Walker?"

Johnson looked over at Detective Thomas who was sitting in on the interview then back at me.

"Officer Johnson, this is Detective Thomas. I believe you have already met her."

"Where did I meet her at?"

"I believe you were with Officer Walker at the firing range."

"Oh, yeah, now I remember her face. She beat Frank.
Boy, what shooting."

"So, we have established that you know Officer Walker now," I said making eye contact.

"How well do you know him Officer Walker?" Thomas asked.

"Hmmm, pretty well I guess," he said.

"How long have you known him and where did you first meet him?" I asked.

He looked at Detective Thomas and then at me. "How did you get someone as pretty as her to partner up with you?"

"Answer the question Officer Johnson," she said looking him in the eye.

"I met Frank, ah Officer Walker two years ago at the Police Academy."

"Were you friends before that?"

"No, I never met him until then."

"Did you get close to him during that time?" Detective Thomas asked him

"Yeah, we grouped up with a couple others so we could get through the academy. Trying to make it through by your self is really rough. Each one of us more or less took on a different roll in the Academy's academic courses."

"After graduation you stayed buddies," I asked.

"Yeah, kind of like blood brothers, you know."

"Do you like gays, Officer Johnson?" Detective Thomas caught him off guard and he had to look down and get himself composed before answering.

"I never thought much about it to tell you the truth."

"What about gay cops?" I countered back at him.

He just looked at me and stared

"Officer Johnson, where were you on the night officer Gomez was killed?" I asked him.

"I was with some buddies of mine hanging out before the shift started. You know, laughing and cutting up most of the day and evening. Why?"

"I was just asking."

"Do I need an alibi Lieutenant? Is this why I'm in here?"

"No, but it helps to better understand where people were and to be able to eliminate them from further talks."

"Well, Lieutenant Wilhelm you can check with my buddies if you'd like. I can give you their names and addresses."

"I would appreciate you getting back with me and give me those names to us." I said looking at him.

If you don't have anything else may I be excused and go back to my duty section."

"Officer Johnson, you are free to go anytime you want,"

I said making sure he looked me in the eye.

"Fine, I want to leave."

"There's the door."

"Well, well, detective you did great with that question. Hit him when he wasn't expecting it on gay cops."

"Think we should check their files for when the two of them were in the academy?"

"Yes, and maybe we might pick a few more names. Let's take a ride pass Linda Gomez's house once again before we call it a day. I want to look around in the back yard for any clues."

"The Wolf is hot on a scent is he?" She said.

When we arrived at Linda's I gathered in more visual information than before. It was still daylight, hot out and dry. No rain for awhile. The house was a small brick structure. It was a single level with three steps up to the porch. There were four rooms and a bath. The driveway was paved like they did years ago. Just the line of where the tires traveled was paved. There was grass growing between the paths.

No one said whether or not Linda drove so I went out to the garage to look around. There was a small twenty inch cut push mower and some small garden tools hanging up. In the center of the garage was a small car. An older one I think. They stopped making that model a few years ago.

"What do you see detective?"

"Everything is where it belongs and nothing out of order."

"Right, so a robbery was not the case here or there would be stuff scattered around."

"Let's look around the grounds in the back while we are back here." she said.

We walked around for awhile looked in the back door and then walked around to the front. A lot of times my returning to the scene of a crime later gives me more insight into what happened. As we walked up the steps and entered I started getting a strange feeling and I stopped suddenly. Jeri ran into the back of me and gave me a shove.

"You're going to need brake lights Wolf stopping like that in front of someone." She said almost tripping.

"Sorry Jeri didn't mean to cause you to trip over me."

"Are you on to something?"

I looked around as we entered the living room. The only bedroom was in the back where Linda was found. Kitchen and small dining room was to my right. The bathroom was between the living room and bedroom.

"Jeri, would you check the bathroom and medicine cabinet."

"What're looking for?"

"Xanax?"

"Okay."

"I'll start in the living room and work my way towards the bedroom. Meet you there," I said.

I checked the drawer in the coffee table and down between the cushions of the couch and chair. No Xanax. I went to the bedroom and waited for Jeri to finish up.

"Are you about through in there?" I said peeking in the door.

"Nothing in here," she said getting up from looking in the bottom of the vanity.

As we walked into the bedroom we could smell the awful odor left from the blood. The bed and been stripped down and the mattress had been flipped over.

"I wonder where her purse is," Jeri said.

"Need to find out."

The house was in a tidy way when the crime occurred and afterwards. The killer or killers didn't even want to make it look like a robbery.

"Call the CSU Jeri and ask them if they picked up her purse along with anything else they might have found," I said.

"Use your cell phone."

I waited until she got off the phone.

"CSU says they never found her purse or her weapon but they checked with the precinct and she checked her weapon in before she left."

"I'm sure she had a back up of her own and probably in her purse."

I was looking in the night stand drawer and discovered a pill bottle clear in the back. Pulling the drawer out farther out and very carefully I looked at it. It was the Xanax bottle.

"Is that what I think it is?" Jeri said coming close to get a good look at it?"

"That's it. The CSU we're looking for anything else after taking one look at Linda's body. Let's look in the kitchen and see what else we can find."

In the wastebasket under some papers there was an empty whiskey bottle. I lifted it out by the neck with my pen and it was a Jack Daniels.

"If the only set of fingerprints on either bottle is Linda's then I think she tried to commit suicide," I said looking over at Jeri.

"Was it that bad working with Walker?" She said

Twenty

One thing about rain you can count on and that's a dreary day and night. This day was no exception. It had been raining all day real hard . . . and the wind blowing. Being in late July it was very hot out with the rain. Steam was coming up off the pavement from the heat making the night a creepy one.

Around two in the morning on a darken street in one of the abandoned old warehouses sat a black caddy with all the windows tinted black. The car was empty now and the occupants were inside. Several minutes later a car with the head lights on low beam drove down the street and stopped and parked behind the caddy.

Two men got out and looked the warehouse over. The brick probably dated back to the early 1900's and most of the windows were broken out from kids with nothing else to do.

There didn't seem to have been any recent activity there except for tonight's meeting. The meeting was for the Blue Society and to discuss the present situation involving the Gomez case and what to do.

The two men entered the warehouse and they could see a single light bulb on above the entrance to the service elevator As they walked across the old floor to the elevator and not making a sound amongst, then got in and went up to the third floor. When the gate opened they could see across the room the outline of a person standing in a door way that led into an office.

There were no windows in the office so there was no need to worry about anyone seeing the lights from the street.

As the two men crossed over to the office there was a man standing outside of it and stepped aside as he done in other meetings. He had on a black hood with slits for the eyes to look out. He also had an M-15A1 carbine in his arms. The room was black except for the two lights that were pointed towards the two men as they entered.

"Have a seat both of you," a voice across the table said.

The two men couldn't make out the voice's looks because of the lights in front of him and he also had on a hood and slotted eyes.

The voice said. "We need to get this Gomez case wrapped up so we can go on with our next purpose that we started. What can you tell that I don't already know?"

"Lieutenant Wilhelm is on the case along with a detective name by Jeri Thomas," one man said with the glare from the lights in his eyes.

"I know that and he's known as the Wolf also. He has interviewed people right now that more or less implicated you."

"We have kept with the case as best we could without showing ourselves."

The voice said. "We need to clean this up and get the Wolf off of it."

"We have a few things we have discussed about the Lieutenant and the detective."

Voice, "Why in the hell did you rape Officer Gomez, did you leave any trace of DNA on her?"

"No, I used a condom," He said. "The bitch deserved it."

"I know what you're saying she was a foxy woman and having to be gay. What a waste," the voice said.

"Yeah, I thought maybe that might throw whoever is investigating off the trail a little bit. She was in a stupor when I got there any way. I knew where she kept the extra door key. She didn't answer the door bell so I went in figuring she might be in the shower or something."

Voice, "Wolf is the best and if he's on the case we have to be very careful. So, clean up any loose ends you two and I'll get back to you."

They had never seen the man with the Voice. They were recruited while at the Academy to join the Blue Society and were each paid ten thousand dollars to do the dirty work for the boss. Their goal was to kill the other three gay cops that came from the academy. After leaving the warehouse they drove to an empty lot to make plans as to how they were going to try and throw the Wolf off the case. What laid ahead for the Wolf?

They had already eliminated one other cop in San Francisco. That was planned ahead of Officer Gomez.

It was simple and quick and carefully planned.

Twenty-one

As Wolf got up in the morning he thought he would give a Jeri a call. See if she might want to meet him at the gym.

After talking to her and agreeing to meet him he packed his gym bag and drove over to the gym. After getting changed and as he was coming out of the locker room he saw her standing at the desk.

"Hey Jeri over here," Wolf motioned for her.

Jeri looked over and waved and started towards him.

"Give me a few minutes to change, Okay?"

I motioned that I would be out in the gym and loosening up some while waiting.

Jeri came out wearing sweats and had her hair done up in a pony tail in the back so it wasn't hanging down in her face.

"Thought we could do some kick boxing for awhile if you don't mind?" I said.

"Are you going to hold the pads for me Wolf?"

"Sure."

The pads were held so a person could kick them and not the person. After working out for about thirty minutes of hard kick boxing we both went to the locker rooms and showered and changed.

We both got back to work we went the coffee mess and each got our coffee. No donuts. Everybody relies on Jeri now to bring in the donuts.

After Jeri entered my office and closed the door. I said. "I looked over Walker and Johnson's academy files and there's something about it."

"What did you find?"

"The first part of the course the two of them were average cadets and then all of a sudden outstanding cadets," I said.

"Why do you suppose that was?"

"Looks to me like some how they started getting help from somewhere."

"From within or outside help," Jeri said looking down at the files lying on my desk.

"Both, but that's my opinion."

"Let's get the academy cadets roster for Linda Gomez when she was attending there and see if we can find something in it."

After pulling the files on Gomez we quickly found out there were thirty cadets in her class. The bigger percentage of those had been men.

We checked her grades and those that were close to Linda's. I let Jeri go over the file to see if she noticed any thing grade wise.

"It looks like there are four or five other cadets with close enough grades as Linda's." she said tracing down the file with her finger.

"I know."

"You know?"

"Yes detective I have already went over her file."

"Then why have me go over her file if you've already done that?"

I told Jeri that she knows darn good and well that if I told her everything she wouldn't learn anything on her own now would you.

"You're right and thanks for letting me have a part of in this investigation."

"Let's take the names of these five and start checking them out," I said.

"Okay," she said. "There are two females and three males."

"How many are close to her age?"

"Hmm let's see now. How about that," she yelled at me. "It shows four of them, three males and the other female."

"All three are in the Chicago area as well according to this Wolf."

"I thought were three instead of four. Where is the fifth?"

"I don't know, Wolf."

"We need to find out where the other male is."

"Maybe he's no longer in law enforcement." Det. Thomas said.

"Just the same, he was in the academy with Officer Gomez and part of the group."

"Let's hope we will find out something when the inquiries come back from other agencies." She said.

"I hope so, because he is a very important person right now and we need to find him."

"Okay detective let's break them down in precincts and go with the one close by first."

"Cadet or I mean Officer Hillary Denham."

"Shall we give her precinct a call and get her work schedule before going to see her?"

"We shall." Jeri said all smiles.

Twenty-two

Officer Denham worked the north side of Chicago and Detective Thomas and I made arrangements with her watch commander at the precinct to interview her.

When she came into the room I could see that she was the exact opposite of Officer Gomez. Officer Denham had no make up on, hair cut very short and was maybe five-five and close to one hundred forty pounds.

I introduced ourselves and asked her to please sit down.

"What do you want with me?" She asked in a husky voice

"So you're the Wolf, eh," Officer Denham said looking at me with a curious frown.

"That's right and we're here to ask you a few questions about your academy days if you don't mind?" I said.

"Just what is going on anyway?" She said looking at us then away.

"You were in Officer Gomez's academy class were you not?" Det. Thomas stated.

"Sure, along with a lot of others," she replied.

"Have you had any contact with her since you both got out of the academy?" I asked her.

"Yeah we try to stay in touch with each other as much as possible."

"You know she was gay?" Thomas said.

"So, what about it," she said looking right at Jeri. "Is it a crime?"

"No," I said. "We have reason to believe that's why she was killed though."

"Do you have anything you could tell us that might help us in this case?" Thomas said leaning over the table.

"All I know is that she wasn't happy in the present situation with her partner."

"How so," I asked.

"Linda said she was frightened about working in her precinct."

"Anyone in particular that she mentioned? Anyone give her trouble officer Denham?" I asked.

Officer Denham looked at me then at Detective Thomas and said. "No."

I could tell she was hiding something from us and was frightened herself.

"Did she ever mention anything about the Blue Society?" Jeri asked her.

"She didn't say anything."

"Okay, I think we have enough from you Officer Denham and thanks for taking time for us," I said getting up.

After she left Jeri looked at me. "She knows more than she told us, doesn't she?"

"I'm afraid so and something has put the fear of God in her. Maybe it could be the Blue Society has already gotten to her and reminded her about Officer Gomez."

"Getting ones throat cut might have an effect, Huh?"

Twenty-three

As we drove back to our station I pulled into a drive thru burger place and we each ordered a burger basket with fries and a soft drink. They didn't have Dr Pepper so I had to settle for a Pepsi.

"You ever think about giving this up and doing something else Wolf?"

"A lot of times but I keep coming back," I said.

"What would you do if you did give it up?"

"I always wanted a cabin in the woods close to a lake where I could go fishing and sleep in as late as I wanted too."

"By yourself, wolf?"

"Well, maybe have a dog to keep me company."

"Oh, I see," she said "wouldn't that get boring not having any one to talk to," she commented.

"I suppose it would after a couple of years."

"What, a couple of years, Wolf?"

I laughed and pulled the Buick out into traffic. I could see her saying under her breath. "A dog."

I dropped Jeri off so she could go into the precinct and write the report of the interview we had with Officer Denham and pulled away.

I parked the Buick and went the station and went into my office and shut the door and went over and sat down behind my desk. I thought about the conversation we had on the trip.

After sitting for awhile and just resting I got up and left my office. I walked over to the coffee mess. I had to pass Jeri's desk on the way. She was busy on the computer filing our report when I leaned over and said. "Maybe I'll have two dogs instead of one."

She turned around and threw a pencil at me then started laughing. I told her I was going to the Dew Drop In later and have a few beers then go home.

I left the building and walked over to the car and a sense that someone was watching me. It started to cloud over and the wind started to pick up.

I called a cab to pick me up instead of driving.

The parking lot at the pub wasn't filled up yet but it was still early. I looked around once again before going in.

I took my usual table and the bartender brought my draft beer over to me and sat it down.

"Is your lady friend coming in later?" He asked me.

"Don't think so tonight."

"Shit, she livens the place up you know."

"Yeah, she sure does that," I said.

Later some bikers came in with their gals and all dressed up in leather, tattoos and body pierced every where. Probably even had them where the eye couldn't see right now. They were an okay bunch, not loud, but just wanted to be left alone. I struck up a conversation with them. You never know when you might need help and having them for a friend is a lot better than against.

They kept buying me beer and once I had two full draft beers brought over at the same time.

They finally got up and left and I decided it was time for me to leave also. The place was so busy one had a hard time hearing himself think. I had a couple gals come on to me but being drunk wasn't the time for me to be with any body right now.

I called a cab because I had no way of getting home. I started out to the cab and the feeling came over me again. I looked up over the top of the cab and I saw a car moving slowly out of the parking lot. I got in the cab and went home.

As I tried to stand still long enough to get the key in the lock I heard a POW! And the porch light above me exploded in my face. I jumped off the porch just as I heard another shot ring out. I stayed down and tried to get to my weapon and looking up as much as I dared to without drawing another shot. It seemed like an eternity before I felt that it might be safe to look up. Whoever shot at me had taken off. I unlocked the door and went inside and called 911 and reported the shooting.

Five minutes later two squad cars pulled up in front of my place. The officers looked around outside and found a set of foot prints across the street and behind a neighbors fence.

I told the officers everything that I could remember and they got in their cars and drove away. Just then a car came screeching around the corner and Jeri pulled her car up to the curb and got out.

"Are you okay?" She asked me running up to the house.

"Yeah I'm okay," I said trying to stand up without swaying back and forth.

"You're shit faced aren't you Wolf?"

"I just had a few beers."

"Here, let me help you get inside and to bed." she said and led me into my house. She helped me to the bedroom.

She helped me sit down on the bed without falling off of it.

Then she pulled my shoes off and my shirt. I stood up and she undid my belt and my pants fell to the floor.

"I usually sleep naked but I don't think I can get my briefs off Jeri."

"I'll pass on that," she said. "You'll have to sleep tonight with them on."

I woke up the next morning with the biggest headache I ever had. I heard a noise outside the bedroom and I tried to get up to see what it was but fell back on the bed. Just then Jeri came in with two cups of coffee.

"How do you feel this morning?" she moved over to the night stand and put my cup down.

"What happened anyway?" I reached for my coffee cup.

"Well let's see. You got drunk and someone tried to shoot you last night."

"Is that why my knees and elbows are so skinned up being too drunk to know enough to catch myself on the ground?"

"They know who it was?"

"No, just a set of foot prints left behind and not clear enough to get a plaster cast of the prints."

"My head feels like hell right now."

"What'd you do last night any way?"

"I remember drinking with some bikers and then taking a cab home."

"Smart thing to do, probably being drunk in this case saved your life."

"I think so. Who put me to bed? What are you doing here so early in the morning any way?"

"I put you to bed and slept on the couch just in case the bad guys decided to come back."

"You took my clothes and shoes off?"

"Yeah, but I wasn't about to help you out of your clothes so you could sleep naked."

"Sleep naked!"

"That's what you said, you sleep naked."

"I don't either, I haven't slept naked since . . . well, been a long time. Let's put it like that."

"Must have been the booze talking them," she said.

"That and having a pretty lady undress me."

"Thank you."

"Thank you for your help and sticking around."

"You would have done the same for me . . . Right?"

"Yeah, but don't tell me you sleep naked."

"Okay," we both stated laughing real hard.

Twenty-four

Later walking around outside Wolf found where one slug had embedded in the trim around the door. Reaching into his pocket he pulled out his pocket knife and began to dig out the slug. After a time of it the slug finally came out and dropped into his hand and he could tell it was smaller than a nine millimeter. It looked like maybe a thirty-eight or even a thirty-two caliber. Wolf felt that the gun itself was small and a second gun.

He knew a few people that worked in ballistics and one in particular that owed him a favor or two. Wolf called him and asked if he brought the slug over if he would get a make on it.

After getting the okay to bring it over he would do the ballistic tests on his lunch hour. This could be a break he was hoping for.

When I arrived at the police station Jeri was busy filing reports to Captain Penney.

"Where have you been?" She asked me looking up from her desk.

"I noticed a place in the door trim of house where there was a slug in it."

I sat down on the edge of her desk and took a piece of candy she had in a jar.

"What you do with it?"

"It was right there in plain sight so I dug it out and took it over to ballistics to have it marked for ID."

"Do you remember how many shots were fired that night?"

"Two I'm sure of."

"So, how's you're the knees and elbows feeling?"

"Sore and skinned up. I was a good target for whoever fired those shots."

Jeri looked at me and said. "If you weren't so drunk you probably would have landed differently."

"Yeah I know." I said. "Landing in those bushes and trying to get my gun out messed me up. Could have been worse and landed in thorns."

"Good thing you had the cops sense of survival."

I told her about the slug being smaller and she agreed that it was from a small easy to conceal hand gun.

I asked her if we had any hits from the other police agencies that we sent out to. After checking again we came up lucky.

"San Francisco has sent information to us telling of a policeman being murdered. It's a male officer in his twenties, single and gay, Wolf."

"How long ago did this happen?"

Jeri looked again at the report in her hand and looked up, started counting her fingers.

"Six months ago."

"Had to use the old finger calculator?"

"Guess what the cause of death was?" She said not commenting on my remark.

"It was one shot to the head."

"So, how did you know that?"

"Lucky guess, men are harder to kill by cutting their throats so gun shot would be my logical guess."

"A thirty-eight, single shot to the temple," Jeri said.

"Why murder, couldn't it have been suicide?"

"No, this says the murder weapon was never found."

I said to Jeri as her head was down reading the report. "That makes sense then."

"Do you think this a connection to our case?"

"Could be about a murder for hire or something like that."

"Says here, that the officer had been drugged and then shot in the head," she said laying the report down.

Wolf had a feeling that this was beginning to be a police thing and that the Blue Society might be mixed up in the west coast killing as well.

We need to run the Officer's name with the other names we have on Linda's classmates in the academy. Find out if maybe there is one more we don't know about.

"Do you have any ideas Wolf? Who might be mixed up in this?"

"None stick out, but someone has the capacity to organize something on this scale. It's too big."

"You're saying that this might go higher that just the street level? I mean someone that wants to kill gay cops in the department? Wolf."

"Let's bring in some other officers and see if we can get any information that might help us."

"You're going to try and get another officer to break the code of the blue? Wolf." She said with a frown. "Break the blue wall down."

Part 2

Twenty-five

Lieutenant Wilhelm knew it would be hard to get one of the blue uniforms to come forward and say anything against another officer. The blue wall was hard to break down when it came to investigating their own. He knew there would be resentment from them. That's why the Lieutenant chose to do the interviews himself and leave Detective Thomas out of the interviews.

Monday morning I got up early and fixed myself a hardy breakfast. I knew this wasn't going to be a good day at the office.

After getting to my office I contacted the shift commander and requested that Officer Dan Tobias be relieved long enough so I could talk to him.

Detective Thomas stuck her head inside my door and asked? "Are you sure you want to do this alone?"

"Yes, I'm sure."

"Okay, you know I will help."

"Thanks," I said as I was getting a ball point pen out of my desk drawer.

Officer Tobias was a stocky guy. He had a bull neck and his arms big from lifting weights. There wasn't a wrinkle in his uniform anywhere. He was a pleasant person to look at and well groomed.

A knock on the door and officer Tobias was shown in by Detective Thomas.

"So, Lieutenant, you wanted to see me?"

"Come in and have a seat. Officer Tobias you went through the academy two years ago or about?" I asked with pad and pen in my hand.

"Me and a lot of other candidates did, why?"

"Did you see or hear of any unusual activity while there.

Approached by anyone or receive any material?" I asked him.

"No, what's this all about any way Lieutenant?"

I looked at Officer Tobias and could tell he was telling the truth.

"We are doing some checking on a complaint filed back a couple of years ago that has resurfaced again."

After talking more with the officer I let him go back to his duty section.

We had three more interviews and nothing. All said the same thing. What ever happened years ago was so secret that only a few knew about it.

I got up from my desk and walked over and opened the door and called Detective Thomas into my office.

"What'd you find out?" she said coming into my office and closing the door.

"I didn't find out anything Detective."

Twenty-six

Beverly Sutton knew she should have told them the truth.

Being scared as she was prevented her from telling the lieutenant and detective. She knew what would happen to her if she would have told them how Linda had been harassed and the things that were said to her. How Officer Walker had repeatedly come on to her and she pushing him off. How she was scared of him.

Now Beverly had to live with herself knowing those responsible for Linda's death were still out there free.

She could still remember Linda telling her how bad it was and hating to go to work.

Beverly went into the kitchen to get her a cold beer thinking if she drank enough she would forget. One beer left. Not enough she said to herself. She had to go to the store anyway so she'd might as well go now and get some more beer while she was out.

The drive at night wasn't what she wanted but the lack of beer made her go. She left the house with all the lights on including the front porch light. The more lights on the safer she felt. She turned the radio on after getting in her car and starting it and drove off. Not much traffic on the road she said to herself.

She pulled into the parking lot of the store and went inside. There were just a few customers shopping. A policeman came into the store and stayed for awhile and then left.

She guessed it was so no one got any ideas to rob the place. She loaded up her cart and went over to the cooler and grabbed two twelve packs of beer. Thinking this should last her for awhile.

While loading the groceries and beer into her car she watched a police car drive by real slow and looked her way. It made her want to get home as soon as she could.

Driving home she looked up into her rear view mirror and saw a police car with their cherry top lights flashing pull up behind her.

"Oh, sweet Jesus now what have I done now she asked herself. If it's a tail light I'll end up getting just a warning." she said to herself.

She pulled over and watched the patrolman get out and walk over towards the car. He looked at the license plate.

Not a big policeman she thought. Not like Officer Walker that is for sure. Beverly reached over towards her purse on the seat to get her drivers license and looking up with her license in her hand and saw the patrolman's name tag.

"Please, no!" She cried out.

He fired one shot into her left temple and lifted his right hand off the roof of the car and walked back to his patrol car. After driving away he called into dispatch and reported he was back on patrol. No mistakes he remembered the voice saying. He had Officer Gomez's back up thirty—eight so nobody could trace the murder weapon back to him.

If only the Wolf hadn't been so drunk the night he tried to kill him. Tonight he made sure things went right . . . or did they?

He went back to see his partner and let him know that the witness had been taken care of. Now they could start making other plans, hoping the boss would finally get off their backs.

Twenty-seven

Wolf had been asleep for maybe two hours when the phone rang. Needing sleep he brushed at the phone and knocked it off the night stand unto the floor. He could barely hear a voice from the receiver, a woman's voice yelling.

"Wolf, damn it would you pick up the phone it's me Thomas."

Looking at the clock Wolf picked up the receiver and phone and said. At 3 a. m. he'd better be important and then he sat up.

"Is Beverly Sutton being murdered, that important enough?" she said.

"Oh, shit! What happened?" I said trying to wake up and stop yawning.

"She was murdered sometime after midnight on her way home from the store. Her car was off on the side of the road and shot in the head."

"Why was she out driving for gods sakes?" detective.

"She went out for some things including beer and on her way home pulled over for some reason."

"Okay, tell me where she's at now and I'll get there as soon as I get dressed."

After telling Wolf, Jeri went back to the crime scene making sure the crime scene was taped off and barricades put up to keep traffic away. Jeri went back to her car and waited.

I got up and went into the bathroom and splashed cold water on my face and combed my hair. I reached for a pair of jeans and a tee shirt that said cubs on it and put them on. I pinned my badge on my belt and checked my Glock 9 and put it back in the holster and secured it in the back of my belt. Grabbing a light windbreaker that said HOMICIDE on the back I went out the door. I drove the corvette.

It was dark out and hardly any traffic on the road this time in the morning.

I spotted an all nighter opened and pulled in and got two cups of coffee and a couple Danish rolls to go.

This was going to be a long day. As I got close I could see the police lights and emergency lights flashing. Parking back away from it all I got out and grabbed the coffee and rolls and walked up to Detective Thomas' car and put them down on the hood of her car.

She came over and I handed her a cup of coffee.

"There's a Danish roll for you also Detective."

"Thanks Wolf I really needed this," she looked up into his eyes and saw something in them that she hadn't seen before, a lot of anger.

"Well, we might as well start," I said.

"Beverly was shot at close range in the left temple Wolf."

We walked over to the car and I noticed that the side window was down.

"Why is her window down do you suppose detective?"

"My guess would be to flag down help."

"Was her car still running when the police arrived?"

"Yes," she said looking around.

"Why would she need help then?"

"What do you think, Wolf?"

"I'll tell you in a minute."

I went over to the car and looked in the driver's side window. I put on rubber gloves so not to contaminate the crime scene. Sticking my head in the window and looking around I spotted something on the floor between her feet. When I opened the door to retrieve the object Detective Thomas put her gloves on.

"Well, well, look here Detective Thomas."

"Her driver's license," she noted.

"Now why do you suppose it was on the floor and not in her wallet?," I asked looking at it carefully.

"She had to have dropped it, but why?"

"Maybe she took it out to show someone and dropped when she was shot."

"So some one she knew or trusted walks up and she takes her drivers license out and rolls the window down and BANG!, She's dead." Jeri said.

"Suppose it was a police car that pulled her over and the officer walks up and shoots her."

"We need to stop this traffic and ask if anybody saw anything."

"We'll stop the traffic going in the same direction as she was. Maybe someone saw something on the way in to town."

After talking to a few people one said he passed a car with lights flashing heading out of town behind another car.

He wasn't sure what the other car looked like. The CSU was finishing up and the assistant medical examiner was having the body bagged and readied for transport to the morgue. An autopsy would be performed later.

"I wonder if it was the police car or a person with a red bubble light that pulled her over," I said looking at the victim's car.

"Person or persons either police or not got her to pull over and then got close enough to shoot her but why?"

"Maybe it was because she knew Linda Gomez, Detective Thomas."

"You mean this was set up to look like a regular hit or robbery, Wolf?"

"Nothing is missing right? Her purse and wallet are still in the car."

"She was our key to Linda's murder."

"Let's go to her apartment and go over it. Maybe we'll find something."

"Wolf."

"Yeah, what is it?"

"Someone had to have known about Beverly and since she wasn't mentioned by name in the papers it has to be a leak from within our own."

"Right Detective and now I think they feel we're getting close."

Checking Beverly's key ring I tried to figure out if any keys were missing but no luck.

Twenty-eight

Two in the morning and it's really dark as. Two guys drive down the dark road amongst the old warehouses. They keep to themselves and look side to side. They know where they're going but always watching for a tail.

The old warehouse was once used back in the prohibition days when bootlegging alcohol was illegal. Trucking the brew as soon as they put it into bottles to try and stay ahead of the G-Men.

Some of the warehouses still have the remnants of the old vats that were used. Ghosts of Al Capone and his men probably still walk around these warehouses. Pock marks here and there from bullets flying back and forth in the old brick.

The two men parked their car and entered. Getting on the elevator and going up to the floor for their meeting with the boss.

Upon getting out of the elevator they could see the lights ahead just as before and entered the room. The lights were blinding them so nobody could be identified in front of them and the boss there. The boss's hands were on the table . . . big hands with a ring on one finger. Johnson looked and tried to figure out what the ring meant. Just then the voice spoke.

"So you two screwed up again. Eh?"

"It's not our fault Wolf was drunk and weaving back and forth when he got back to his place," spoke up one of them.

"Now he is more than ever cautious of his actions now making it difficult to take him out," said the other one.

"What about the Sutton woman?" The voice asked.

"We took her out yesterday and made it look like some one shot her while stopping to help,"

None of them knew about the driver's license found on the floor.

Voice: "So, you just pulled her over and walked up to her car and shot her, just like that."

"She didn't even know what was going on . . . she thought it was a routine pull over."

Voice: "I have another job for you and I hope it goes better than the first."

After getting their instructions the two of them left. There was something about the ring one of them saw but if he mentioned it to anyone he would surely be killed. He thought he would wait and see what he could find out about the ring. May be he would use the knowledge of who it belonged to for his own monetary means. Sooner or later the voice would be his to do with what he wanted.

Patience he told himself. He knew one thing he had to get enough prove so he could use it and it required absolute secrecy.

Even his partner wasn't to be trusted. For now planning for his future was going to be on his mind and making sure the boss wouldn't come back on him.

Twenty-nine

Detective Thomas wasn't too thrilled about going back to Beverly's apartment but she knew it was part of the process. Get use to it she told herself.

As the both got out of the Buick Wolf couldn't help it but notice several Latinos hanging around. I looked at the one I figured was the ring leader and called out to him.

"Hey there, would you watch my car while I'm in the apartment?"

The Latino looked at the others and started laughing then they all started laughing and pointing towards me.

I walked up to the ring leader and motioned for him to come close to me. The tattooed ring leader pointed back at him as if to say, "Me." I nodded to him.

I took him aside and whispered something to him and he looked towards Detective Thomas. The smile the Latino had disappeared. Then he looked back at me and nodded and walked away.

I started walking towards the apartment entrance as Thomas hurried and followed me inside.

"What was that all about out there Wolf and why look at me?"

"I told the ring leader you were a black belt and if anything happened to the car you would be more than glad to dislocate a few joints, meaning body wise. I also told him it was a police car as well and he would be healing in jail for along time if something happened to the car."

"Why, do I get the sense that something is always about me" she asked.

"Don't know, maybe because I like you and I know I'm not lying about your abilities. Besides he knew it was an unmarked police car and he thought he was going to have some fun in front of his gang."

Of course the elevator still wasn't working a grey haired lady was trying to pull a shopping cart of laundry up the stairs. Jeri saw Wolf go over to her and say something then took out a piece of paper from his jacket pocket and wrote something down. He said something to her and she replied back. She smiled and we walked around her and on up the stairs to Beverly's apartment. The stairs was so cluttered with trash and wine bottles.

"What Wolf?"

"She told me who the Landlord is and I told her I would see to it that the elevator was fixed."

We reached Beverly's floor and nothing had changed as far as the clutter and smell in the hall. I knocked why I don't know. We knew she was already dead. Guess from habit. The next door neighbor came out and said Beverly wasn't home. We told her what had happened and if she could let us into her apartment. She went back to get a spare key but by then I had turned the door knob and found the door wasn't locked. We drew our weapons and moved into the apartment very slowly and taking one room at a time. Nothing . . . the neighbor came back with a spare key and found us already in the room.

The apartment had been trashed and someone went over her place real good. The TV was gone and her jewelry.

The murderers were looking for something and made it look like robbery. Whoever shot Beverly removed her apartment key and came back to look for something. Maybe there had been a letter or something. The motive wasn't robbery that was for sure.

Detective Thomas looked at me and thought of something. "Why go through all this if it's robbery they wanted. Why not just follow her home and then rob her?"

"You and I both know Detective, robbery was not the intent."

"Someone wanted this to be confusing and throw us off the real meaning for her death."

"Exactly, they wanted to shut her up. She knew something and they weren't taking any chances."

"What's that noise Wolf?"

"I don't hear anything."

"Listen."

"A whimper of some sort but where . . ."

"Here Wolf under the sink," Jeri knelt down and opened the doors under the sink and there cuddled up and shivering laid a puppy.

The pup was about ten weeks old and looked like a German shepherd.

"Well, well, detective look at there."

As I reached in the pup growled and showed its teeth, I pulled back.

"You try Jeri."

"Me."

"Sure, maybe he or she doesn't care for the male gender."

Detective Thomas reached in real slow and careful not to upset the pup. The puppy put its nose up to her hand and started licking it and its tail was wagging back and forth.

"Looks like you have a friend," I said.

The pup came out and looked at me and the hair on the back of the pup stood up. Wolf stuck his hand out and spoke to it and then he turned his hands palms up and spoke again. The pup then walked over to Wolf and licked his hand.

"What did you say to the pup Wolf? Whatever It was made the pup change its mind about you."

"It wasn't what I said but what was in my eyes that the dog understood. Dogs know fear, anger and love by the way humans look at them. Soothing voice and eyes that tell a dog it's going to be alright will calm a dog down. at least a pup . . . takes longer with a grown dog."

"Let's look around some more then leave. I don't think we'll find anything," She said.

I picked up the pup and held him under my arms and we left.

The gray haired lady was just coming onto the same floor with her cart as we went by.

"I see you found Baron," she said and petted the dog.

"Everybody loves Baron."

"How long has Beverly had the dog?" I asked her.

"Oh, about a week I guess."

"We didn't see it when we last saw her." I said.

"We would take turns watching him so the landlord would never find out about him."

We left and the gang was gone also. The car was okay and a note was left under the windshield wiper.

"Tell the lady detective with you to have a nice day." signed Ice.

I showed the note to Jeri and we both laughed. We got in the car and left.

Thirty

We went back to the precinct to file our report and talk to the captain.

As we walked up to the door Officer Thompson came out and started to say something to Detective Thomas. Baron started squirming and I put him down. He went over to Officer Thompson and sniffed him and then raised his leg and peed on his shoe. The look on Thompson's face said it all.

"You know Baron I am going to really like you." said Det. Thomas.

We walked in the door and up to my office. Baron was right next to me and looking around but staying close by. He went over to Jeri and stayed close to her.

Once in my office I went over to my desk to fill out the report. We could hear Officer Thompson and then a whole lot of laughter.

Captain Penney came out of his office and walked by Detective Thomas and headed for Wolf's office. He tapped on the door and went in and closed it behind him.

"Cap." I said as I looked up.

"Wolf, we need to talk."

"Okay cap, now what?"

"There's been another."

"What?"

"You know damn well what," saying in a loud voice.

A low growl came from behind the desk.

"It seems Baron doesn't like loud voices," I said.

"Is that the dog that peed on Thompson's shoe?"

"Fierce isn't he," as I picked him up and showed Baron to the captain.

"Wolf, another police officer died last night."

"Where'd this happen at Cap?"

"It happened on the north side."

"Have you got a name?"

"Officer Terrance Monroe. He hasn't been with the force for very long."

"Let me guess, as long as Linda Gomez."

"I don't know about that."

"Hang on Captain," I got up and went over to the door and opened it and called Jeri to gather her notes and come into my office.

"Detective Thomas has been doing the research on the class that Officer Gomez was in at the academy."

"What's the name?" She asked as she pulled out the file with the names on it.

"Terrance Monroe," I repeated.

"Let's see here, Gomez . . . yep, Monroe was in the same class." she said.

"So Captain, fill us in."

Baron went over to Jeri and sat down under her chair.

"They said maybe he over dosed."

"Does the Medical Examiner have him now Cap?"

"Dr. Hagan does."

"What brings you in here with the news Cap?"

"Officer Monroe was gay."

'Uh huh, maybe the Captain's starting to see some thing we've been seeing."

I filled the captain in on everything including Walker leaving out nothing and including the driver's license that I found in Beverly's car.

"It's got to be more than just one or two," he said.

"I'm afraid so and the detective and I are trying to figure who that person might be."

"Johnson has an alibi for the night Officer Gomez was killed?" Cap asked.

"Yes, and it checks out."

"What about Officer Walker, he wasn't too fond of her from what I've read in the reports?" The captain said.

"We'll get back to you Cap as soon as we come up with more information."

"Mean while Wolf we need to go see Dr. Hagan don't we?" Thomas said.

"Excuse us cap."

We got up and walked out with baron between us. The other officers yelled Officer Thompson's name and pointed at Baron. He looked up and threw his hands up and sat back down.

Dr. Hagan was in her office when we got there. A lot of certificates on the wall and her desk stacked up with folders of autopsies done and to be done. She met us at the door and offered us something to drink. She didn't have to ask me what I wanted. She knew Dr Pepper and diet coke for Jeri. Dr. Hagan went over Officer Monroe's prelim with us and the fact he had over dosed.

"How long had Officer Monroe been using drugs?" I ask her.

"This was a first time."

"You don't say. No other marks?" Jeri asked.

"No and if he used the same entry point he would have black and blue bruise marks. No other bruise marks any where else before you ask."

"Was he drugged first?" I asked.

"Possibly, he had on rubber gloves."

"The toxic tests won't be back for awhile but I'd say he was drugged."

"Thanks doc."

"Let's go detective."

"Where now, back to Monroe's place?"

"Exactly," I said to her.

"Wolf, if Linda and apparently tried to commit suicide then why the same means to drug Officer Monroe?"

"It's no secret among cops what Xanax and alcohol will do. Linda helped the killers by taking the drugs herself and being semi—unconscious at the time the killers entered her house. They not knowing of her attempted suicide and killing her before the drugs did making it murder. Linda had given them what they wanted.

"This is the one thing that we don't want anyone to know about. If it gets to the top man then his plans might change," Thomas replied.

"Exactly, this will be the one clue not on any report and used only by us until we need to bring it to any one's attention."

"Won't the killer be surprised to know he could have waited and the drug doing his job for him. Could have been easy money for him had he known."

"Jeri, the killer had it in for Linda Gomez so I believe even if she had been found dead by him he would have left some kind of statement behind."

"Who could have that much hate and resentment?"

"The killer's that's for sure."

Thirty-one

Officer Monroe's apartment on the north side was nice. Well kept and tidy. The neighbors thought he was an okay guy. He always kept to himself, and always waving to them. His apartment was on the first floor side entrance. The night of his death neighbors said he had come home with another guy. A good friend he told everyone he saw that night that he had not seen in a long time.

We were going to get photos of the other suspected gay cadet that went to the police academy the same time Gomez and Denham. We now had a good idea who number four was. How was Officer Monroe drugged and who could have gotten close enough to do it. Another policeman was a possibility.

One thing for sure we needed something positive to go on. These people were good enough to stay ahead of Wolf but soon he was going to put it all together. A second person had to have gotten into Officer Monroe's apartment.

The only person was the friend that the neighbors saw. One neighbor remembered the two coming back around 8 p.m. and then the friend leaving about eleven but then seeing a guy or guys he wasn't sure coming to the apartment around 1 a.m.

The neighbor remembers because he fell asleep on the couch watching television and getting up to go to bed. He heard a car and a few voices and they got out an entered the apartment. The neighbor didn't see them come out.

Nothing until the cleaning lady came by this morning. A shrill scream from her brought everyone out of their apartments.

We went over the crime scene and noticed that the coffee table in the living room was moved out away from the couch. There had been a needle, rubber band and traces of heroin on the table when the CSU got there.

His body was found lying on the floor beside the table. Rubber gloves were found on the victim hands. This meant that there weren't any possibility of finger prints on the needle. How smart of them. Cause of death . . . a question mark.

This was very clever thinking into making this look like a suicide attempt. Now it was up to us to prove it wasn't a suicide but murder. Could the friend shed any light on this case and bring the photos here so the neighbors could get a good look at them.

Thirty-two

The captain called me on my cell phone and told me that there was going to be a press conference and for me to be there tomorrow at 9 a.m. out in front of city hall. The major, police chief, district attorney and police superintendent were all going to be there. I could hardly wait.

"Now the press is putting pressure on city hall and wanting answers," I said.

"Bout time," remarked Jeri.

We got back in the Buick and Baron nuzzled up to Jeri and we left Monroe's apartment.

"What now?" She asked.

"I'm going to take the pup home but first stop and get some puppy chow. Then go and get me something to drink."

"You mean like beer? Drop me off back at the station so I can get my car."

"Want me to pick you up later, say around seven."

"Sure, why not."

I pulled into the stations parking lot and waited till she started her car then the both of us left.

I stopped at a convenient store and picked up some things including puppy chow. Once home I fed Baron and stripped off my clothes and took a hot shower. The water felt good and I wanted to relax and enjoy the night. Tomorrow would be quite a day I was afraid of. After getting cleaned up and putting on some after shaved straightened out Baron's bed again and changed the old towels I had found. I decided to take the corvette tonight.

Taking the t-tops down me then got in and looked up and saw all the stars shining.

I parked out front of Jeri's and walked up to her house. Nice home, very old looking brick with a fireplace at least there was a chimney indicating one was there. There were flowers, shrubs and a small tree out front. There was a large porch in front, and a swing at one end. I rang the door bell several times, no answer. Just as I was going to bang on the door again it opened.

"Wolf, you sure do get impatient when no one answers the door, don't you. Come on in. Want something to drink?"

"No thanks."

Her place was really nice. There was a fireplace, cherry wood furniture and thick white carpet. There were pictures of mom and her father and her late husband on a stand. I picked it up and looked at it.

Jeri had returned to her bathroom to finish whatever she was doing before I got there. When she came out she was gorgeous. Her hair was blond and beautiful. Eyes and make up just right. One word was all I could think of . . . Wow.

"Well, how do I look? Okay for tonight."

"You look great Jeri."

"Thanks." and she kissed me on the cheek. We both hugged one another and I knew we'd better get out of here real fast. I took her to a real nice steak house and enjoyed every one staring at us, or Jeri I should say. One half the steak house was for dining and the other half had a bar and music.

We were seated at a nice table with a red table cloth and a candle in the middle. The candle was lit and we ordered our meal. We both had a red wine to go with our steak. After eating we went into the other half of the restaurant and were shown to a table away from the bar. It suited me just fine.

I ordered drinks for us, gin and tonic for Jeri and Southern Comfort and seven up for me.

She caught me looking at her.

"What?"

"Oh, nothing, just thinking to myself," I said.

"And what might that be you're thinking?"

"I saw the picture of your parents and your late husband back at your house," I said looking at her.

"Wolf that picture is still there because my parents still want to think of him. I've let go awhile ago but my parents haven't. I forgot to take it down after they left the last time they were here to see me. They really liked Michael,"

Jeri said as she put her hand on mine. "They haven't gotten Michael out of their system yet."

"Thanks Jeri for going out with me tonight. I'm lucky to have someone as beautiful as you with me, considering."

"It's me that's lucky to be with you."

"You being a bachelor like yourself and having a reputation for criminal investigating."

"I guess we're both lucky then."

"Yes we are both lucky."

"The case has me on edge Jeri. I know there is something I'm missing and not being able to put my finger on it."

"Wolf, forget about the case for at lease a couple of hours. Okay, and let's enjoy tonight together."

"Okay. I do enjoy your company Jeri and you working with me."

"Really Wolf."

"You're smart, intelligent, well educated and . . ."

"Whoa, enough."

"Are you ready to leave Jeri?"

"I'm ready whenever you're ready. I'm with you tonight."

I paid the check and left a big tip. We walked out into the cool night air. As we walked to the car I reached for her hand and then pulled back away. Jeri reached for my hand and looked at me.

It's okay, I'm over it."

I opened the car door for Jeri and as she started to get in I reached for her and kissed her.

"Thanks." she said looking up at me.

When we arrived back at her place I excused myself and asked to use the bathroom. When I came I looked over at the stand. The picture that had been there before was no longer there. I looked over at Jeri and saw she was closing a drawer to one of her end tables.

"There." she said.

Thirty-three

Jeri turned on the radio and a country and western song was playing. It was Hank Williams Jr. One of his that goes good with beer, pool and a pretty lady.

Jeri came over to me and asked if I wanted anything

"No," I said and pulled her close to me and kissed her full on the lips.

She drew back and looked at me. "Well Wolf, what was that for."

I drew her close again this time she put her arms a round my neck and drew herself up on her tip-toes. The kiss was longer, hotter and a lot of tongue by both of us.

"Wow, Wolf," she said as she pulled back just enough to look up in my eyes. "Let's do that again."

I slid my hands down along her back and grabbed the cheeks of her butt and squeezed then let go then rubbed her butt up and down with my hands. Jeri mean while was trying desperately to get my sports jacket off. I was rubbing her back and she finally got my jacket off and started on my tie and unbuttoning my shirt. I reached up and found the zipper to her dress and pulled it down.

All this going on while the two of us tried to stay in our kissing. Jeri took me by the hand and pulled me towards the bedroom. Once in there the two of us undressed each other in such.

I tried to undo her bra reaching around her but having no luck. She finally laughed and undid it herself. Her breasts were absolutely beautiful and just the right size for me. We finally stripped off our clothes and crawled in to bed. The sheets and pillow cases were a dark red and made of silk . . . curtains to match. That's about all I noticed with her there with me.

I reached over and placed my hand on her breast a cupped my hand around it. I leaned over and started licking her nipples. She let a soft whimper and slid her hand down and took a hold of my manhood and slid her hand up and down then squeezed it sending hot streaks up me. I ran my hand down across her belly and on down finding her hot and wanting me inside her. My finger felt hot and wet. She pulled my hand away and kissed me with a lot of passion.

I rolled over on top of her. As she spread her legs so I could put myself inside her and the pleasure that ran clear through me was great enjoying this moment. Moving up and down together slow . . . fast . . . faster until both reached a monster of a climax.

Both of us out of breath I glanced down at Jeri and kissed her again and again. My hands were moving all over her breasts.

I was looking at Jeri and said. "We shouldn't be doing this. We're partners."

"We sure are."

Later we had sex again and I finally got up and was looking for the clock and said. "Jeri this was a great date and one I enjoyed and will always remember.

"Me too . . . and one of your wishes has come true you know."

"What's that?"

"You've got a dog to go with your cabin on the lake now." and laughed.

"Right," I said and leaned in the bed and kissed her again and again and then rolled on top of her once more.

Thirty-four

The next day wasn't so pleasant. Arriving at city hall I went around to the side entrance. I could already see the TV and radio trucks setting up out front for the news conference. As I got inside the city hall I was ushered inside the Mayor's office. Captain Penney was waiting for me and told me he had already brought the mayor up to speed except mentioning Walker and his dislike for Officer Gomez. Mayor Kilpatrick came out and shook my hand as others filed out of his office also.

"Wolf, is there anything new to report?" He asked me.

"No, wished there were."

"Time to step outside for the news conference," the mayor's aid said.

"I'll do the talking and let the chief of police answer questions," the mayor said and "Don't take any questions any of you. Okay?"

"Okay." we all answered back.

The aid went first and made a few comments before the mayor and all of us then followed the mayor out onto the steps of city hall. The news hounds were all over the grounds and even on top of some of the vans. There were microphones and cameras, news media trying to push and shove their way to the front.

The mayor spoke and informed the news media that an on going investigation was being conducted and that there were a few leads they were pursuing. He told them the chief would try to answer any questions but was limited to the amount of information he could give out.

The Mayor excused himself and went back in to city hall followed closely by his aid. The Chief stepped up to the microphones and all hell broke loose.

The news people rushed to the chief and some even tripped and fell forgetting the steps up to city hall. Yelling, hand waving and interruptions during the answering session brought a stiff comment from the Chief for all to settle down.

One wanted to know who was the leading investigator and was it true that Lieutenant Wilhelm had been mentioned.

No comment, no comment, no comment was coming out of the Chief's mouth. You would think that the news people would learn what questions would bring a comment but no they kept asking leading questions and getting a no comment.

The conference broke up and the news people were still yelling when the Chief and the rest of us went back inside.

"Whew, what a mob," the Chief said.

"Maybe someone ought to do a report on the way the media acts before, during and after a press conference," I said.

"Be interesting to see and everyone else to see including themselves," Cap said.

Thirty-five

Later that evening Jeri and come over to my place and we sat on the couch together with Baron in between us. The news was coming on and the news conference was the hot item.

Jeri and I watched closely and as the camera panned around we both saw two policemen standing in the background. There were others but those two stood out. Why?

Who was Johnson's partner and why was he always alone.

I wondered why I never see Johnson with his partner. He was always alone. It was time to find out.

Baron was content and asleep between us so putting my arm around Jeri was impossible. After all she showed up saying she came over to see the dog. Poor excuse but it worked.

We ordered out for pizza and when it arrived I was cautious when I opened the door. I looked around out side while paying the delivery boy. I tipped him and he left. The pepperoni pizza tasted good and one look over at Jeri and I started laughing.

"What's so funny?" She said looking puzzled.

"You've got pizza sauce on your nose."

"Want to lick it off?"

"Sure," I leaned over the table and with her eyes closed I licked off the sauce.

"The news conference looks like a mob gone wild." Jeri said, looking at the news conference on television.

"You should have been there. Even the superintendent was there."

"The mayor really didn't give the press much information did now did he."

"Not much to give."

"If only the murderer or murderers had left some thing. Like fingerprints . . . or anything."

"Bingo!" I said letting out a howl.

Jeri jumped and Baron barked.

"What Wolf?"

"Fingerprints, that's what has been bothering me."

You have just solved half of our case."

"What'd I do?"

"We need to get back to Walker's statement on the Gomez case and get Beverly's dusted for prints."

"Beverly's car was dusted,"

"I want the whole left side from rear bumper to car door including the roof dusted. I've a hunch and if it's right we've got our murderers. Call Dr. Hagan and ask what caliber handgun killed Beverly. I'm betting the same as the slug I took out of the door casement at my place . . . a thirty-eight."

"Yes, but we carry 9 mm, all of us."

"Do you carry a backup Jeri?"

"Sometimes, oh Wolf, now I know what you're getting at."

"Exactly, a backup was used to kill Beverly and used to try and kill me. It's all fitting together now and I'll bet the gun belonged to Officer Gomez."

We went into the bedroom together leaving the pup outside the room. Baron went over by the closed door.

Thirty-six

The case was starting to make sense now. With
Walker's statement in front of me I thought I knew who killed
Officer Gomez.

"Just as I had suspected, the report back on the autopsy and
ballistics confirmed a thirty-eight was used on was taken from
my door casing. I felt we now had enough to go after Walker and
Johnson.

I called down to the watch commander and requested that
Officer Walker report to my office.

Officer Walker was outside with Johnson when his two way
radio sounded.

"Officer Walker, would you please report to Lieutenant
Wilhelm's office."

The two looked at each other and Officer Walker turned and
walked back into the precinct.

When he got to the Lieutenants office he looked over towards Detective Thomas but she was doing her best to ignore him.

One rap and he entered. "What's up?" He said coming straight towards my desk.

"Sit down Officer."

Walker stopped and gathered himself in and sat on one of the chairs.

"This won't take long Officer and then you can go back to your duty section. I just want to make sure all the reports filed on the night of Officer Gomez's death by our attending uniforms are correct."

"Don't have anything else to add to my report and I told you everything."

"You entered the rear of the house?"

"That's right, just like I said."

"Where were you the night Officer Gomez was killed?" I asked him.

"I was with a bunch of guys at a pool hall playing pool. Why?"

"I was just checking all the Officer's statements."

"I would have told you that the first time you had me in here but you didn't ask me."

"How many were there at the pool hall at the time you were there?"

"Oh, maybe six or eight guys including the bartender and a waitress."

"Okay, you can go."

Detective Thomas came into my office after Walker had left. "That was quick," she said.

"I thought I gave him just enough rope to hang himself, instead he has an alibi."

"I still don't understand, Walker and Johnson having alibis."

"Jeri, the labs report on the Gomez crime said the only prints taken were that of the police."

"I know that."

"Walker said in his statement that he had to enter the house from the back door he found open."

"Go on Wolf."

"He said he pushed the door closed with his elbow so not to leave contaminating prints on it."

"But the door was open when we went around in the back that night."

"Exactly, and I'll bet someone's prints are on the inside door knob when he used it to open the door."

"Who set the crime scene up Wolf? Are you saying someone else was there instead of Officer Walker?"

"Walker had to have gone in the back door like he said to check the crime scene and make sure everything was in its place."

"They were there and killed Gomez before the drugs did."

"Yes damn it! Walker and Johnson both have alibis and it pisses me off." Wolf then threw a pencil across the room in frustration.

Thirty-seven

He had been standing back from the crowd during the news conference. There were so many news people and unruly at that. He watched the Mayor give out information and scanned over the rest of those in that were there. Mayor, Captain, the District Attorney, Superintendent and Wolf, then something caught his eye.

There was something shining from someone up there. Getting a little closer he saw what it was. It was a RING.

Now he knew who belonged to the voice and he began shaking and went back to his patrol car. Now how was he going to use this piece of luck?

That night he and his partner were called to the warehouse.

Voice: "So tell me about Officer Monroe."

"We went over to Monroe's place under the pretext that we had information on Gomez's murder and we needed his help. He let us in and I put my gun to his head while Johnson here tied him up. All we did then was fix him up with an over dose of heroin.

Voice: "Okay, good now go back to work and stay out of trouble. I'll let you know when I need you again."

He stared at the ring and now he had a face to go with the ring. It was black onyx with small diamonds in the shape of a star in the middle.

He had never seen a ring like that before so this had to be the person he saw at city hall. Now what he asked himself?

As the two were leaving the warehouse he was trying to figure out how to use this new discovery for his own use.

First he was going to write something down and put the notes away for safe keeping. The two left the warehouse figuring things were finally starting to go their way.

Little did they know the "Wolf" was now on their trail?

Thirty-eight

Beverly's car had been dusted for prints just like Wolf wanted and now the results were in. One set on the left rear fender above the wheel well and another on the roof above the driver's door. Killer didn't have a care in the world when he strolled up to her car putting his right hand on the car. With his right hand on the roof he leaned into the car and shot her.

Wolf remembered now the killer had to be left handed. His nine mm was on the left side and baton and flash light on the right.

It was time to bring him in and question him about Beverly's murder. Wolf had enough probable cause to detain him but Wolf wanted the big fish in the pond.

He was going to meet the Lieutenant at a place they both agreed on.

It was a small bar just off the main drag. They were both dressed in casual clothes. The bar was small time with a pool table, juke box but no place dance. Two guys were throwing darts and arguing over the score. What was in and what was out.

One female was sitting at the bar with a cigarette in the ash tray burning and trying to bum another one from the bartender. She looked like the old saying 'rode hard and put up wet.'

Wolf sat in the back and when he came in he ordered a draft beer. Taking it with him he walked back towards Wolf's table.

"So what do we do now Lieutenant?"

"Pull up a chair Johnson," I said. "I'm not going to mince with the words so listen closely. I'm going to give you a chance to come clean or charge you with Beverly Sutton's murder. Take it or leave it."

"You're fucking crazy."

"Am I?"

"You don't have anything against me and you know it."

"Tell me Officer Johnson, how well do you know Beverly Sutton's car?"

"Never seen it or been around it. Why?"

"Funny, then how come there were two distinct sets of hand prints on her car and both belonging to you?"

The expression on Johnson's face and the way he swallowed told me he was guilty.

"I don't know what you're talking about."

"Officer Johnson your left handed and the one that killed Beverly is left handed. The night she was murdered someone walked up to her car putting his right hand on the fender and the roof of her car. Also there is a thirty minute lapse in your call in. Dispatch confirms that you went thirty minutes off the radio."

"So, I got a bite to eat and went to the john."

"When did you get close to her car?"

"I never did,"

"Think about this. You have twenty-four hours to come clean or face a murder charge. What I want from you is the person in charge of the group called the blue society."

"What society, Lieutenant?"

"Remember, twenty-four hours."

He left knowing that the Wolf was close, very close.

Thirty-nine

Wolf decided to take Baron with him to the precinct this morning and stop by and get some doggy treats.

When he pulled into the parking lot and got out Baron was already bristled and hair standing up on his back. Wolf gave him his freedom to wander and he went over to a squad car and started growling at it. Wolf tried to pull him away from the car but he pulled himself back towards it. Wolf read the car number to himself and went in to the precinct.

Wolf called Detective Thomas into his office and asked her to check the squad car number he gave her. Later she returned with the information.

"The squad car belongs to none other than Officer Johnson," she reported.

"I figured it to belong to one or the other."

I told her about the meeting with Johnson and that he denied having any knowledge of Beverly's death.

"I'm going to see Captain Penney and bring him up to date on Johnson," I said looking down at Baron but talking to Detective Thomas.

"When I come back I hope to the green light to haul Johnson's ass in."

Later Wolf was told by Captain Penney that Johnson was not to be brought in but would have a surveillance put on him. Word came from upstairs and who it was from he didn't know.

I wanted a search warrant for Johnson's place but was turned down by the district attorney, not enough evidence I was told for the warrant.

"What now Wolf?"

"We hound Johnson for the right now and talk to his partner. Maybe he'll shed some light on our boy."

Johnson's partner told us that he was always given things to do around the precinct by Johnson and then he would go out on his own.

Forty

Johnson knew the ring and the person that was wearing it. He wanted out of all this because the Wolf was closing in and he wanted to get away. Some where far away and he needed money to do this. The heat was coming down and was going to make to make the voice pay dearly.

He looked the ring's telephone number up and called from a pay phone.

A young secretary answered the phone and said that he wasn't free but if he'd hold she'd put him through as soon as he was free. He told the secretary to mention his name. A few minutes later Johnson was talking to the voice he had heard many times at the warehouse.

Voice: "How can I help you Officer Johnson?"

Johnson: "Cut the crap you know who I am and now I know who you are. You're the one in the warehouse with those bright lights in front of you."

Voice: "Officer Johnson, I believe you have the wrong number and the wrong person."

"I want out and two hundred thousand dollars to keep my mouth shut or I tell the wolf about you and you're recruiting Walker and me from the police academy to do your killing for you."

"I can't discuss anything over this phone but if you would like to meet me some where then maybe we could iron this mistake out."

"Call me on my cell phone."

"Give me your number and we'll try to work this misunderstanding out."

"Okay, here's my number, call me or else."

Voice: "Are you threatening me?"

After talking later on his cell phone Johnson set 1 a. m. as the time to meet and at the usual place.

He met the voice out front of the same warehouse they had used previously for the meetings. They both walked into the warehouse together and up the elevator. In the office they both sat down across from each other at the table. Johnson's hand was on the thirty-eight in his pocket all the while.

Voice: "What are we to discuss again . . . money?"

Johnson: "That's right, two hundred thousand dollars and I disappear or I tell the Lieutenant who you are and all the plotting by you to have us do your killing."

"Oh but you don't have any proof do you?"

"I have more proof than you think. How do you suppose I knew whom to call?"

Voice: "What proof are we talking about, tell me."

"Let's just say it's a little something that will put you a way for a very long time."

"It will take awhile to come up with that kind of money."

"You have until midnight tomorrow."

Johnson got up and left the office and went down the elevator. As he walked to his car he looked down at the damp pavement and opened the car door.

Voice: "Let him get a couple of blocks away before you detonate the car," he told the person that had ridden in the trunk of voice's car.

Johnson's car pulled away and went on down the road.

"Okay now?"

"Yeah it's okay."

A big explosion and a giant mushroom ball of fire rose up where the voice could see and turned and shot the man standing there beside him between the eyes. He just eliminated Johnson and one other one that could incriminate him.

There was only one other person left and he wasn't about to come forward.

Forty-one

Wolf received the call early in the morning from Detective Thomas and hurried to the scene. Police cars, medical examiners car and EMT's were already present.

"Ambulance is on its way," said one of the attending officers. "No rush for this one."

There wasn't much left of the car. It was torn in half and both pieces still burning. The middle part of the car was gone. There was metal thrown everywhere. Tires were burning, rear axle and bumper lying in different places on the pavement. Part of the left door was visible with an emblem on it. Cicero Police Department was barely showing on the car door, the rest burnt black from the blast.

"Any ideas as to who the driver was?" I asked walking up to the scene.?

It was still a hot scene so everyone had to stay back until the fire department contained the fire.

"We think it was Officer Johnson's car. He had reported going off radio communications for about thirty minutes," said one of the officers.

"He came back on the air about 25 minutes ago, then nothing. Dispatch tried to contact him but no answer." Det. Thomas said.

"Is there enough to ID the person?" I asked Dr. Hagan walking over to her.

"I don't think there's enough of him left to put in a pill bottle but we'll do our best."

"This isn't making any sense Wolf,"

"It seems the Blue Society has lost one of their members Detective and I'm wondering if Johnson tried to leave it and was killed because of it."

"Did someone know of your meeting with him and had him taken out?" She replied.

"One thing for sure, he knew the big boy. He's toast now maybe because of greed."

"It looks like we're back to Walker now."

"We might as well let the CSU and Dr. Hagan alone to do their jobs and let's go and get some coffee and breakfast."

I had the Buick so I followed Jeri back to her place so she could leave her car and ride with me. I was driving to a place to get something to eat my cell phone rang.

"Hello . . ., yes this is Lieutenant Wilhelm. What! Who is this? Yes I can hear you."

"Who is it?" Jeri asked.

I waved her to be still. "You want to meet me. Yes I will guarantee your safety. Just say where and no one in the precinct will know you called. Hello . . ., Hello."

"You'll never believe who that was Jeri."

"Okay, who was it?"

"Johnson."

"Johnson!"

"Yep, our boy Johnson is still alive and wasn't in the car after all."

Forty-two

"We're to meet him on the west side at a small park tonight after dark. He'll call us and let us know which park and what time later."

"What do we do Wolf, ride around on the west side and wait for his call?"

"Think of anything better to do right now Jeri?"

"Uh huh,"

"What?"

"Nothing." and she laughed.

The phone started ringing and it was the call we'd been waiting for and the puzzle was fitting together. The park wasn't too far from where we were so I told Johnson we could be there in ten minutes.

The park was small with one street light over the swings and the slide. A couple of old picnic tables and an old basketball court now broken up with weeds growing up out of the cracks in the asphalt. I pulled up and Johnson jumped in the back seat.

"Keep on driving," he said.

"What happen?"

"Just drive and I'll tell you the whole story," he told us.

Before he spoke me had Detective Thomas read him his rights under the law? With that understood a small tape recorder was laid on the seat and turned on.

He told how Officer Gomez was killed and who it was. They had found her in a stupor. When she didn't answer the door bell they used the extra key over the front door to get in.

That's when the killers found her like she was.

Johnson went on and said that the killers were paid just like he and Walker. They were members of the 'blue society' also.

The killers came out later with blood on their arms and hands and said they finally done the bitch in. They also told how one raped her then grabbed her and pulled her head back and cut her throat.

"Officer Johnson, what did the two guys look like?"

"I don't know they had funny masks on when they came out and had Linda's purse with them and then that's when we found the thirty-eight inside.

Johnson said that he and Walker didn't kill Officer Gomez. They waited outside for the others to come out.

He went on to tell how Walker opened the back door to enter and make it look like a break in.

Later the two of them left her place and returned to Walker's pad. He had his uniform on and returned to the scene only to report a break in and a murder.

Johnson told how he and his partner were recruited at the academy and what they had to do in order to belong to the 'Blue Society.' Plus their grades were altered so they would be sure to graduate.

I kept trying to get him to name the big boy but Johnson just kept talking so I finally let him talk.

He told us that it was he that tried to kill me at my place and shot Beverly Sutton.

Walker killed Officer Monroe. He went over to his apartment and telling him he knew who killed Linda Gomez. After Monroe let him in Walker drugged him and made it look suicide. Johnson kept on talking. He told of the meetings at the warehouse and how he finally figured out who their boss was.

The night of his car blowing up he figured some thing was up when he looked down on the ground before he opened the door. He thought something likely was going to happen to him. That's why he took precaution when he left the building.

He also told of calling the boss and arranging the meeting and how much he'd ask for and how there were marks on the ground like someone had been under his car while in the meeting.

There was a bum walking down the street so he gave him ten bucks with ten more to follow if he would drive his car around the block and come back to pick him up. He saw the explosion and ran as fast as he could away from the warehouse.

They threatened Officer Denham over the phone and that's why she wasn't co-operating when she was interviewed.

The puzzle was now almost complete and Wolf wanted the final piece.

Walker's statement to me was that he saw the back door open so he went in using his elbow to push the open enough for him to get through.

The fingerprints that came back were from police officers including the back inside door knob that Walker used to open from the inside. This was what was bugging me when Jeri mentioned fingerprints the night we were eating pizza. Walker had to have been inside her house not outside like he said.

Johnson told how they arranged for the Officer in San Francisco to be killed also. He was in the grad class along with Linda Gomez and the others and had been put on the list to because he too was gay and from the academy.

When he told us his name I knew the name now from our list we had received from the San Francisco police department.

He told how he saw a ring on the boss's finger at one of the meetings and took a voice activated tape recorder to the last meeting for insurance sake. He knew then he had him because he recognized the ring on the person during the press conference held outside city hall and put two and two together.

I couldn't wait to arrest the man responsible for the killings. I wanted to bring an end to the blue society.

Finally Johnson told me and Detective Thomas the name of the owner of the ring and his boss. We could not believe our own ears.

The man knew things were getting unraveled by the Wolf. With Johnson out of the way he could come up with a plan to escape. He had to contact someone first.

Someone he knew he could trust. One that owed him a favorite and now he was going to collect it.

Forty-three

I met with Captain Penney and played back the tape of the conversation we had with Officer Johnson. I told him that I had Detective Thomas read him his rights before the confession and that I had Officer Johnson in a safe place for now.

Captain Penney after hearing the tape said he would arrange for a meeting at City Hall.

First the "Wolf" wanted to bring in Officer Walker.

The lieutenant called Detective Thomas and told her to meet him at the precinct and be sure to have her vest on. When asked why the Lieutenant told her they had the go ahead to arrest Officer Walker.

Officer Walker wasn't at the precinct when Lieutenant Wilhelm arrived. Detective Thomas met the lieutenant outside and informed him Officer Walker was not to be found.

"Have dispatch try and get a hold of him" he told Detective Thomas.

Detective Thomas went back inside to make the call. When she came back out she looked at Lieutenant Wilhelm and shook her head.

"He's not answering his radio Wolf." She said.

"We're going to go look for him." I told her.

"Do you know where he might be?" she asked me.

Just then the dispatcher came over the radio and said Officer Walker was spotted leaving his apartment and was heading towards the warehouse district.

He was in uniform and driving his patrol car.

Wolf advised all units to be aware of Officer Walker and that a warrant for his arrest was being issued at this moment.

Consider Officer Walker armed and dangerous Lieutenant Wilhelm said over the radio.

"Where do we go now, Wolf?"

"We're going back to the warehouse where Johnson's car was blown up."

"Do you think he would go back there?"

"They said they spotted him heading that way so we'll take a look and see."

Turning the corner and coming around where Johnson's car had been blown up . . . Wolf could see a squad car parked outside the warehouse.

"Be very careful Jeri and stay close to me."

They pulled up outside the warehouse and got out. Jeri came around the car and stood beside the lieutenant.

"Do you have your vest on Wolf?" she asked him looking at him.

"I put it on when we were at the station." He replied.

Wolf pulled his weapon out of the holster and slid the barrel back putting a round in the chamber. He made sure the safety was on and put the weapon back in the holster.

Detective Thomas did the same.

"Okay, we're going to go in and try to talk him in to giving himself up. I don't want to have a gun fight with him."

"He is very good with a gun Wolf." Detective Thomas said.

"I know and that worries me."

Inside they both looked around could see that it had been a long time since any activity had gone on there. There were old boxes thrown around and windows broken out. There was a path that had been made to the elevator and the Lieutenant and Jeri walked down it to the elevator. Just then they heard noises coming from up above.

"Okay Jeri, be ready for anything and for God's sake be careful."

"I'm with you Wolf."

"HELLO! Officer Walker can you hear me. This is Lieutenant Wilhelm speaking. Why don't you come down here so we can talk to you?"

"Go ahead and get in the elevator Jeri."

Wolf got in behind her and slid the big gate closed. The elevator started upward and as it came to the second floor Wolf pushed Jeri to the side.

He opened the gate and walked out into the open area. The whole floor was empty. There was no place to hide. Wolf got back on the elevator and started up to the third floor.

Wolf heard a noise on the third floor and coming to a stop he motioned for Jeri to crouch down with him as they got off.

"WALKER!" Wolf yelled and there was a slight echo. "We want to talk to you."

"Go away Wolf!" Officer Walker said.

"Come on Walker give it up."

"I'm not going back with you so you'd better leave." He said.

Wolf motioned for Jeri to move around some boxes and he was going to try and get closer to Walker if he could. He moved and Walker fired his gun at him. "WOLF" Jeri cried out. "Are you alright?"

"Yeah, He missed me."

By then Wolf had his weapon out and was duck walking around some other boxes when another shot rang out. He ducked down even more. He came to a wall and pushed some boxes over to be able to slide along the wall.

There was another shot fired and this time it hit right above him and sent pieces of concrete in his face. Wolf started around some more boxes and Walker was waiting for him. Wolf not knowing where Walker was kept walking and as he turned the corner Walker was aiming his gun at the lieutenant.

"Well, Wolf it looks like your sniffing days has come to an end." Walker said.

Wolf couldn't do anything. He was caught off guard.

Walker pulled the hammer back on his weapon and a shot rang out. Wolf looked at Walker and saw the blood start to run down his chest where his heart was.

Walker looked down at his chest and fell.

I looked around and saw Jeri holding her gun. It was still pointed at Walker.

"It's okay now Jeri, He's dead."

Jeri handed me her weapon and let out a big breath of air.

"Walker forgot that there was a better shot than him up here." I said looking at Jeri. "Thank you for saving my life."

"I couldn't save Michael but I could you. I didn't want to lose another person that I love so much."

"Let's call it in Detective Thomas."

"What will you do now Wolf?"

"I'll call it in and let the CSU come out and process the crime scene and then I'll make out the report."

"They'll be an investigation on whether or not it was a justified shooting or not, but that won't take long."

"Let's get to city hall so we can get the boss of this ring."

Forty-four

He called all those that were present for the news conference to be there at 9 a. m. tomorrow morning.

City Hall was buzzing as usual this morning but it was going to get real busy soon.

Those that were to attend the meeting in the mayor's office were;

Mayor Kilpatrick. A tall slim person, red headed Irishman in his early forties. He was wearing a grey suit with a blue shirt and grey tie. He was over six feet tall.

The second, that was to attend, was the District Attorney, Charles Clarkson, a no—nonsense DA. He was short, pudgy and bald. He and the mayor were always joking about their difference in size.

The DA had on a black suit, white shirt and black tie. He was close to fifty, a late bloomer as far a DA goes but the last election he and the mayor ran on a rid-the-city of crime ticket.

The third one, the Captain, he was in a brown suit, brown vest and white shirt and multi-colored tie. He also had on his wing tip shoes. The first time I had seen his brown ones.

Fourth, was Chief of Police, Donald Foreman, six one, two hundred. He was an ex-boxing champ and wearing his chief's dress uniform. Very impressive I had told him. All his medals he had on were deservedly earned.

The last to attend was the Police Superintendent, a man that had stated many times of his desire to see the just get justice and the innocent to always be free of reprisal. Superintendent Allen had a deep voice and was in his dress uniform also.

The ribbons and medals on his chest were impressive and well earned. His fellow Officers on the force admired him and respected him.

He was over six-two, weighed close to one—ninety, well educated and came from a well to do family. His hair was the color of a silver fox.

Wolf knew the boss of the Blue Society was soon to be surprised and his coming arrest unexpected. With all this in mind Captain Penney was about to inform those in attending of the facts and evidence leading to the arrest.

Once everyone was in the room Captain Penney realized that the Mayor's aid was not in the room. The Captain had the aid summoned to be present. The aid, small wimp like, white as chalk came into the meeting. No suit jacket on, tie loosened around his neck.

Now that everyone was there in the Mayors office

Captain Penney made the announcement that Officer Johnson was alive and now had come forward and confessed to his part in this bazaar case.

A police officer came into the room and gave the captain a note. Captain Penney read it and looked up.

"Can I have your attention." he said. "This note I have here says that Officer Walker was killed in a gun fight with Lieutenant Wilhelm and Detective Thomas."

Lieutenant Wilhelm walked into the room with Detective Thomas and introduced her to everyone.

The room became a bee hive with all the buzzing going on. Everyone was talking at the same time. I looked over and one person looked worried.

"Officer Walker was responsible for the cold blooded murder of Officer Monroe and an accessory to the death of Officer Gomez. He also was responsible for the death of another officer in the San Francisco police department."

Wolf walked over to the door and leaned against it so no one could leave.

Then Chief Penney said. "The one most responsible and the leader of the Blue Society is here in this very room right now and he is wearing a diamond studded star ring."

The Captain moved swiftly over to the Superintendent Joseph Allen and said. "You are under arrest for conspiracy to commit murder," and as he said that an officer moved in behind the superintendent and grabbed his left hand and raised it showing the diamond star ring.

He was now handcuffed and the "Wolf "was asked to read him his rights. He then turned him over to the officer to lead Joseph Allen out of the room down the hall, out of City hall.

He was led down the steps to a waiting police car. Oddly enough it was Officer Tobias that led him out.

Somehow the press had caught wind that there was going to be some thing big going on at City Hall and if they wanted the news of the century they'd better be there. They were and Allen was lead right down passed them. He was protesting loudly as he was placed in the squad car. Screaming "I'm innocent, don't you know what they're trying to do to me."

Forty-five

Back at the precinct all was quite the next day. Except . . .

"Lieutenant Jonathan Wolfgang Wilhelm will you please come to the conference room," came across the PA system.

Wolf got up and along with Baron and headed for the conference room. Upon opening the door to the room he heard a loud cheer and saw a banner hanging that said.

"Congratulations Captain Wilhelm."

Captain Penney came over and reached for my hand and said. "Cap. Congratulations."

Baron was growling and then his tail started wagging when Jeri came over and picked him up.

"Well Wolf?" Jeri said.

"I don't know what to say."

"Some day soon for the both of us," she said.

A. W. Hopkins

"Soon," I said putting my arm around her and letting Baron lick me on the cheek, real soon."

"Three cheers for the Captain," everyone said.

Later the news came out that Superintendent Allen had hung himself in his cell where he was being held. He had ripped the sheets into small strips and wove them together making a very nice rope . . . no note.

I always wonder even to this day why Joseph Allen had not been placed on suicide watch.

This had another bazaar twist to this case. Whether or not the 'Blue Society' was indeed stopped was unknown for now but hoped for. Time would tell.

Forty-six

Captain Wilhelm put only one more year on the force and then retired. He was given a years credit for the solving of the high profile case. Wolf and Jeri were married and retired to a cabin on the lake along with Baron. Wolf still does consulting work with the police department when he finds the time. Lately he hasn't found much time.

The Blue Society wasn't heard from again. Not in Chicago at least. Corruption in City Hall stopped for now. Officer Johnson was convicted of murder and was given the death penalty. He is still on death row.

The other hooded person never was identified and was still at large.

Officer Denham testified that she indeed had been threatened over her cell phone and traced back to Walkers' cell phone.

There was no emotion out of Johnson when he was informed that Officer Linda Gomez had committed suicide and was probably minutes from dying of an overdose when she was killed.

A dead body was discovered by a homeless person in a warehouse. Gun shot to the head. The Body was too badly decomposed to be identified. No identification was ever made as to the person in Johnsons' car when it blew up either. Officer Monroe's funeral was the same as Officer Gomez's. There were no frills but the attendance was by far great in number.

As to the final gay person, his name was never mentioned and was allowed to remain silent. His career went on unblemished.

Superintendent Allen. People forgot he and his wife had an only child, a son. Everyone was led to believe the son was off in Europe somewhere but in fact died two years ago from HIV.

He had contracted it from a blood transfusion. It was suppose to be a simple operation, one pint of blood and the loss of his only son.

Allen vowed then that he would do something about it. He was going to avenge his son's death because of a gay person donating the blood. Given enough time he would come up with a plan and would send a clear message to all gays not to join the police force in Chicago.

Forty-seven

The lake was clear as a mirror and the trees were turning colors now. Reds, yellow, gold, all beautiful. Baron was grown now but still had the puppy in him and he enjoyed his time walking with Jeri and Jon. The Wolf's name was now put to rest by Jeri. She called him Jon and he liked it. They enjoyed the lake and she was glad that he finally got all his wishes to come true. While Jon was sitting outside in the swing Baron was running and chasing squirrels up the trees.

Jeri came out with the telephone in her hand.

"Call for you," she said handing him the phone.

"Who is it?" Wolf said reaching for it.

"Don't know the voice."

I put the phone up to my ear, "Hello."

"Just wanted to say hi from the Blue Society" the caller said.

"Who is this?"

"You don't know me for now anyway." the voice said then hung up.

"Who was that?" Jeri asked reaching for the phone.

"Someone making a crank call I guess."

"Wait a minute. No one knows our phone number except for Captain Penney."

Was the Blue Society stopped? Was there someone out there higher up or someone that just wanted it all to stop and had information to bring it to a close. It left Wolf puzzled.

There hadn't been anybody convicted for Officer Gomez's death. Surely this wasn't him that called.

"Come and sit with me for awhile Jeri."

She went over and sat down. I put arms around her and kissed her and told her how much I loved her.

"What's going on Jon? Is there trouble?"

"I don't know. I need to call Cap and ask him some questions. Be right back."

Wolf got up went into the house and called Captain Penney.

"Captain Penney, Homicide Division," he answered.

"Cap, Wolf here."

"Hello Wolf, glad to hear from you."

"I'm calling from a secured phone line Cap."

"Just a minute and I'll transfer this call to my secured line."

The captain went over and made sure the door was closed and then came back to the phone.

"What do you need? It's been a while since I last talked to you. How's Jeri and of course the dog?"

"Everybody is okay. I received a call a little while ago from someone that got a hold of our phone number."

"How could that be? I haven't given it out to anyone."

"Whoever called got our number and called saying he was with the Blue Society or knew something about them."

"When is this going to stop?" the captain said.

"I don't know if he is the other man that wasn't identified in the murder of Linda Gomez or not."

"Do you still think Allen was the top dog Wolf?"

"Yes, I'm sure of that and I am going to try and set a trap for this other person out there."

"How are you going to do that?"

"We'll see Cap, we'll see, thanks Cap and take care, always watch your back."

"I all ways watch my back any more, and good luck. Tell Jeri I said Hi."

When he came back out Jeri asked him. "What did you find out?"

"Cap doesn't have any idea how my number was breached."

Baron came over and laid his head in Jeri's lap and looked up at her and we both hugged him, and he sat back down and let out a big sigh as if to let us know all was well.

Forty-eight

Jeri had some errands to run so she went down to the grocery store there at the lake. On her way out she always picked up a newspaper for Jonathan. This time the headlines almost made her drop everything. She rushed home and ran in the cabin yelling, "Wolf, Wolf."

"What is the matter?" Wolf yelled out with Baron on his heels.

She ran up to him and handed him the paper. "Here look at this," she said almost out of breath.

The paper fell to the floor trying to hand it to him and scatted on the floor.

Both of them bent over to pick up the paper and put it together so he could look at it.

"What's so important?" He said finally getting the paper back together.

The headlines read the headlines," Jeri said.

Wolf opened the front section and his mouth fell open.

Cicero Chief of Police John C. Penney found dead in his home.

Wolf couldn't believe it. He sat down to read the rest of the article while Jeri looked over his shoulder.

Chief John C. Penney apparently died of a massive heart attack.

Wolf got on the phone and called Chief Penney's wife and expressed how sorry he was to hear the news.

She told him she wanted to call him but her husband kept their number to himself. She also told him of a note in his wallet saying that if anything happened to him he wanted you to investigate the cause.

"A massive heart attack isn't something to investigate is it?" Jeri asked.

"It's been a long time since we've seen him so I don't really know how his health has been. He's never mentioned anything to me what little conversation we have had back and forth. Just the other day I talked to him about my number being used."

"What now? Are you going to leave here and go back to work on this?"

"Not right now. I'll wait awhile and see what happens. There ought to be an autopsy and I'll wait for the results. I'll phone Dr. Hagan and ask her to pass the results on to me if there's any fowl play involved."

They both sat and stared at the paper neither one saying much. The days passed by and finally the call came from the medical examiners office. They said they would fax the results to Wolf. The results showed no fowl play and that Chief Penney did indeed die of a heart attack.

Wolf lost a close friend and the fact Chief Penney had a premonition that something would happen to him didn't make him feel well.

Would the feeling go away he had and the feeling his close friend had as well. Give it time he told himself, give it time.

I want to thank Ian Marlowe and the staff at universe Publishing Company. Without them this book would have never been a reality for me.

Watch for the next book on Wolf's adventure into the underworld of crime.

This book is made up of fiction story telling and although Chicago is a real city and the streets and Mac Neal hospital also.